SHAKEN

SHAKEN

A Jack Daniels Thriller

J.A. KONRATH

PUBLISHED BY
amazon encore ≋

The characters and events portrayed in this book are fictitious. Any similarity to real persons, living or dead, is coincidental and not intended by the author.

Published by AmazonEncore
P.O. Box 400818
Las Vegas, NV 89140

3 1558 00299 5561

ISBN-13: 9781935597216
ISBN-10: 1935597213

From the Author

This book was deliberately written out of sequence. Normally, thrillers are linear, following a single timeline. With *Shaken*, I jump backward and forward in time, with a structure more like a crazy quilt than a straight line. This allowed me to explore Lt. Jack Daniels at various stages in her career, comparing who she once was to who she would ultimately become.

I'm pretty sure my readers have the mental prowess to follow this skewed timeline.

Also, there's an author afterword that's worth checking out, to help prepare you for the next Jack Daniels novel, *Stirred*. It explains a bit about the ending, and where the series is headed next.

As always, thanks for reading. I hope you have as much fun with this one as I did.

Joe Konrath
Schaumburg, IL

Twenty-one years ago
1989, June 23

*T*his *guy isn't a killer,* Dalton thinks. *He's a butcher.*

Dalton isn't repulsed by the spectacle, or even slightly disturbed. He stays detached and professional, even as he snaps a picture of Brotsky tearing at the prostitute's body with some kind of three-pronged garden tool.

There's a lot of blood.

Dalton wonders if he should have brought color film. But there's something classic, something pure, about shooting in black and white. It makes real life even more realistic.

Dalton opens the f-stop on the lens, adjusting for the setting sun. He's standing in the backyard of Brotsky's house, and his subject has been gracious enough to leave the blinds open. From his spot on the lawn, Dalton has a clear view into Brotsky's living room, where the carnage is taking place. Though Brotsky has a high fence and plenty of foliage on his property, he's still taking a big risk. There are neighbors on either side, and the back gate leading to the alley is unlocked. Anyone could walk by.

It's not a smart way to conduct a murder.

Dalton has watched Brotsky kill two hookers in this fashion, and surely there have been others. Yet the Chicago Police Department hasn't come knocking on Brotsky's door yet. Brotsky has been incredibly lucky so far.

But luck runs out.

At least Brotsky has the sense to put a tarp down, Dalton thinks.

He snaps another photo. Brotsky's naked barrel chest is slick with gore, and the look on his unshaven face is somewhere between frenzy and ecstasy as he works the garden tool. He's not a tall man, but he's thick, with big muscles under a layer of hard fat. Brotsky sweats a lot, and his balding head gives off a glare which Dalton offsets by using a filter on his lens.

Brotsky sets down the garden tool and picks up a cleaver.

Yeah, this guy is nuts.

Truth told, Dalton has done worse to people, at least as far as suffering goes. If the price is right, Dalton will drag someone's death out for hours, even days. But Dalton gets no pleasure from the task. Killing is simply his business.

Brotsky is killing to meet baser needs. Sex. Power. Blood lust. *Hunger,* Dalton muses, taking a shot of Brotsky with his mouth full of something moist.

If Brotsky sticks to his MO, he'll dismember the girl, wrap up her parts in plastic bags, and then take her severed head into the shower with him. When Brotsky returns, he'll be squeaky clean, and the head will be gone. Then he'll load the bags into his car and haul them to the dump site.

Dalton guesses it will be another eleven minutes. He waits patiently, taking occasional snapshots, wondering what Brotsky does with the heads. Dalton isn't bothered by the heat or the humidity, even though it's close to ninety degrees and he's wearing a suit and tie. Unlike Brotsky, Dalton doesn't sweat. Dalton has pores. He just never feels the need to use them.

Exactly eleven minutes and nine seconds later, Brotsky walks out his back door, dressed in shorts, sandals, and a wrinkled blue Hawaiian shirt. He's lugging several black plastic garbage bags. The man is painfully unaware, and doesn't even bother looking around. He walks right past Dalton, who's hiding behind the girth of an ancient oak tree, gun in hand.

The hit man falls into step behind the butcher, his soft-soled shoes silent on the walkway. He trails Brotsky, close as a shadow, for several steps before jamming the Ruger against the fat man's back. Brotsky stops cold.

"This is a gun, Victor Brotsky. Try to run and I'll fire. The bullet will blow your heart out the front of your chest. Neither of us wants that to happen. Do you understand?"

"Yes," Brotsky says. "Can I put down these bags? They're heavy."

Brotsky doesn't seem frightened, or even surprised. Dalton is impressed. Perhaps the man is more of a pro than Dalton had guessed.

"No. We're going to walk, slowly, out to the alley. My car is parked there. You're going to put the pieces of the hooker in the trunk."

Brotsky does as he's told. Dalton's black 1989 Eldorado Roadster is parked alongside Brotsky's garage. The car isn't as anonymous as Dalton would prefer, but he needs to keep up appearances. The wiseguys he works for like Caddys, and driving the latest model somewhat compensates for the fact that Dalton isn't Italian.

"Trunk's open. Put the bags inside and take out the red folder."

Brotsky hefts the bags into the trunk, and they land with a solid thump. The alley smells like garbage, and the summer heat makes the odor cling. Dalton moves the gun from the man's back to his neck.

"Take the folder," Dalton says.

The light from the trunk is sufficient. Brotsky opens the folder, begins to page through several eight-by-ten photos of his two previous victims. He lingers on one that shows him grinning, holding up a severed leg. It's Dalton's personal favorite. Black and white really is the only way to go.

"I'm a schoolteacher," Brotsky says with the barest trace of a Russian accent. "I don't have much money."

Dalton allows himself a small grin. He likes how Brotsky thinks. Maybe this will work out after all.

"I don't want to blackmail you," Dalton says. "My employer is a very important Chicago businessman."

Brotsky sighs. "Let me guess. I slaughtered one of his whores, and now you're going to teach me a lesson."

"Wrong again, Victor Brotsky. See the lunch box in the corner of the trunk? Open it up."

Brotsky follows the instructions. The box is filled with several stacks of twenty-dollar bills. Three thousand in cash, total.

"What is this?" Brotsky asks.

"Consider it a retainer," Dalton says. "My employer wants to hire you."

"Hire me for what?"

"To do what you're doing for free." Dalton leans forward, whispers in Brotsky's plump, hairy ear. "He wants you to kill some prostitutes."

Brotsky turns around slowly, and his lips part in a smile. His breath is meaty, and he has a tiny bit of hooker caught in his teeth.

"This employer of yours," Brotsky says. "I think I'm going to like working for him."

Present day
2010, August 10

The rope secured my wrists behind my back and snaked a figure eight pattern through my arms, up to my elbows. Houdini with a hacksaw wouldn't have been able to get free. I could flex and wiggle my fingers to keep my circulation going, but didn't have a range of movement much beyond that.

My legs were similarly secured, the braided nylon line crisscrossing from my ankles to my knees, pinching my skin so tight I wished I'd worn pantyhose. And I hate pantyhose.

I was lying on my side, the concrete floor cool against my cheek and ear, the only light a sliver that came through a crack at the bottom of the far wall. All I had on was an oversized T-shirt and my panties. A hard rubber ball had been crammed into my mouth. I was unable to dislodge it—a strap around my head held it in place. I probed the curved surface and winced when my tongue met with little indentations. *Teeth marks.* This ball gag had been used many times before.

My sense of time was sketchy, but I estimated I'd been awake for about fifteen minutes. The first few had been spent struggling against the ropes, trying to scream for help through the gag. The bindings were escape-proof, and my ankle rope secured me to a large concrete block, which I felt with my bare feet. It was impossible for me to roll away. The ball gag didn't allow for more than a low moan, and after a minute or two I began to choke on my own saliva, my jaw wedged open too wide for me to swallow. I had to adjust my head so the spit ran out the corner of my mouth.

Based on the hollow echoes from my sounds, I sensed I was in a small, empty garage. Some machine—perhaps an air conditioner or dehumidifier—hummed tunelessly in the background. I smelled bleach, a bad sign, and under the bleach, traces of copper, human waste, and rotten meat. A worse sign.

Fighting panic and losing, I made myself focus on how I got here, how this happened. My memory was fuzzy. A hit on the head? A drug? I wasn't sure. I had no recollection of anything leading up to this.

But between the smells and my past, I knew whoever abducted me was planning on killing me. I used to be a cop. Now I was in the private sector.

And this was definitely not the way I wanted to end my new career.

Twenty-one years ago
1989, August 15

I didn't become a cop to do things like this.

The red vehicle pulled up and honked at me. It was one of those strange combinations of a car and a truck; I think they were called SUVs. This one said "Isuzu Trooper" on the fender. I found them to be too big and blocky, especially for an urban setting like Chicago. And with gas prices up to almost $1.20 a gallon, I doubted the trend would catch on.

The night was hot, humid as hell, and I was sweating even though I was nearly naked. My candy apple red lipstick kept smearing in the heat, forcing me to reapply it. I had the whole block to myself, having chased the other girls away earlier. I'd done them a favor; action was molasses slow. Plus, the city was eight days into a garbage strike, and the stink coming from the alley was a force of nature.

"Your call, Jackie," my earpiece said. My partner, Officer Harry McGlade, waited in a vintage Mustang parked up the street.

"Aren't you bored with this game yet?" I said into the microphone, which was hidden in my Madonna push-up bustier—an item that should have been worn under a top, not as a top. *Jacqueline Streng, working girl.* I reached inside the cup and readjusted my boob. The transmitter was the size of a pack of cigarettes, but harder and heavier, the sharp corners not meant to be wedged tight against delicate female anatomy. It hurt. The wires trailed up my bra strap, and to the earpiece, hidden by my Fredrick's of Hollywood blonde Medusa wig.

"I'll be bored when I'm actually ahead a few bucks," Harry said. *"Go on. Guess."*

I squinted at the guy behind the wheel. The street was dark, but he had his interior light on while he looked around for something. Possibly his wallet. Hopefully not a straight razor or an Uzi. He was Caucasian, late forties, balding, thick glasses. White collar, probably married with kids.

"BJ," I said to Harry.

"Naw. I'm guessing something pervy."

"He looks like a member of the PTA."

"The clean-cut guys are always the perverts."

"You said the weird-looking guys are always the perverts."

"They're pretty much all perverts. I'll say foot fetishist."

I actually didn't know what a foot fetishist did. Something to do with feet, I assumed, but what? The Vice training manual didn't explain that particular kink. I wasn't about to ask Harry, because he'd make fun of me. It was hard enough being a female in the Chicago Police Department. Being a young female who did prostitution stings made me an easy target for potshots.

Not that I would be young for much longer. Today officially began the last year of my twenties. I was going to celebrate the happy occasion by watching TV and getting drunk. My boyfriend, Alan, was out of town on a business trip, and so far he'd neglected to get me anything. Big mistake. True, I didn't want any reminders of my rapidly retreating youth. But we cops were big on intent. And forgetting your girlfriend's birthday said a lot about your future intent.

Not that I had any intentions myself. His last name was *Daniels*, for chrissakes. I had a hard enough time getting respect on the Job. If my name was Jack Daniels, I'd be the laughingstock of the city.

"You in or out, Jackie?"

"Fine," I said. "Ten-spot?"

"Make it twenty. I got a feeling."

Bald Guy honked again. I pulled up the elastic top of one of my black fishnet stockings, pulled down the hem of my hot pink spandex micro-mini skirt, and walked over to the car on painfully high, strappy heels, trying to look sexy when I felt completely ridiculous. His window opened, and I stuck my head inside. The air-conditioning bathed my face, cooling the sweat on my brow and upper lip.

"How are you tonight, sugar?" I asked, smacking my gum.

Bald Guy appeared nervous, jittery. Most of them did. Maybe because soliciting sex was embarrassing. Or maybe because they were worried that the hooker they propositioned was actually an undercover cop.

Imagine that.

"How much?" he asked without looking at me.

"How much what?" I asked.

"How much money?"

In order to make a clean arrest, and avoid the dreaded entrapment defense, the suspect had to be the one to bring up the subject of money. This guy cut right to the heart of the matter. Now he needed to mention what he wanted in exchange.

"Depends," I said, playing coy. "What is it you're looking for?"

"Something special. Can you quote me your, um, rates?"

"Sure. Head is ten. Straight is fifteen. Half-and-half is twenty. Round the world is thirty. Anything to do with feet is fifty."

"No fair!" McGlade yelled in my ear. *"You're price-jacking!"*

I hoped Bald Guy didn't hear that, even though it was so loud my eyes bugged out.

"I've got kind of a strange request," Bald Guy said.

I leaned in further. The air-conditioning was wonderfully frigid, and the interior smelled like lemon air freshener. After four hours on the street, this was a little slice of heaven.

"Kinky is extra. Tell me what you need, big boy."

"Actually, I'll pay you fifty dollars if you just hold me for ten minutes."

I blinked. "Hold you?"

He nodded, his face puppy dog sad.

"We can't arrest him for that," Harry said. *"Ask him if he wants to suck your toes."*

I ignored Harry, which wasn't the easiest thing to do. Especially with him in my ear. "That's all?" I asked Bald Guy. "Just hold you?"

"That's all." His shoulders slumped. I felt kind of sorry for him.

"Tell him you've been on your feet all day," Harry said, *"and your toes are really sweaty and stinky."*

I wished I could turn the earpiece off.

"That's kind of weird," I told the guy. "Don't you have a mother or an aunt or someone else who can give you a hug?"

"No one. I just got divorced, and I'm all alone."

"How about friends? Neighbors? A church group?"

Bald Guy shook his head.

Harry said, *"Try taking off your shoe and sticking your foot under his nose."*

"I just need a little tenderness," Bald Guy said. "Will you do it?"

He looked so devastated, so desperate. Plus his vehicle was air-conditioned and smelled nice. What more prompting did I need? I walked around the front of his car/truck and climbed into the passenger seat.

"Dammit, Jackie! Find another john!" Harry, screaming in my ear. *"There aren't any laws against cuddling! Don't waste our time!"*

The earpiece really needed an off switch. In fact, so did Harry. The sad thing was, Harry wasn't as bad as some of the other jerks I had to work with. What did a female cop have to do to earn the respect of her peers in this city?

I guessed it wasn't dressing up as a hooker, hawking BJs.

"Okay," I said. "One quick hug. On the house."

I opened up my arms, ready to embrace this poor clod, and he handed me a latex glove. I backed off a notch.

"Are you sick?" I asked. "Contagious?"

"No, no, nothing like that. While you're hugging me, I'd like you to stick your fingers up my bottom."

No wonder he was divorced.

"And wiggle them," he added.

"Mirandize that pervert," McGlade said. *"I'll call the wagon and be right there."*

I opened my silver-sequined purse, reaching for my badge and handcuffs.

"I'm a police officer," I said, making my voice hard, "and you're under arrest for soliciting a sexual act. Put your hands on the steering wheel."

Bald Guy turned bright red, then burst into tears. "I only wanted a little tenderness!"

"Place your hands on the steering wheel, sir. And for future reference, fingers up the wazoo really don't qualify as tenderness."

"I'm so lonely!" he sobbed.

"Buy a dog." An unwelcome image popped into my head, of this pervert with some poor schnauzer. "On second thought, that's a bad idea."

Bald Guy moaned, wiped his nose with his wrist, and then flung open his door and ran like hell. Which didn't make much sense, considering that in jail he could probably find someone to fulfill his request for free.

"He bolted!" I yelled to Harry. "Coming your way!"

I pushed open my door and scrambled after him. Three steps into my pursuit I broke a heel and almost fell onto my face. I recovered in time, but my speed was drastically reduced. A penguin on stilts would have been faster and looked less clumsy. I wasn't about to kick my broken pump off—this wasn't the nicest part of town, and I didn't want to step on a dirty needle.

"He ducked down the alley, Jackie!" Harry said. *"It lets out on Halsted. Run around and block his exit!"*

Easy for him to say. He was wearing gym shoes.

I rounded the corner, hobbling as fast as I could, my spandex skirt riding up and encircling my waist like a neon pink belt. My purse orbited my neck on its spaghetti strap, and each time it passed in front of my face I reached for it and missed. Inside was my Beretta 86, and I didn't want to be charging into any alleys without it firmly in hand.

Honking, from the street. I wondered if it was the squadrol—a police wagon that picked up and booked the suspects we caught on this sting. No such luck. It was a carload of cute preppy guys. They hooted at me, pumping their fists in the air.

"*What's that sound?*" Harry said. "*You watching* Arsenio?"

I skidded to a halt at the mouth of the alley, tugged down my skirt, and pulled out my Beretta.

The hooting stopped. I heard one of the preppies yell, "The whore is packing heat!" and their tires squealed, their car rocketing away.

"Where is he?" I said into the mic.

"*If he didn't come out on your side, he's hiding in the alley somewhere.*"

"I'll meet you in the middle."

"*It's dark. Don't shoot me by mistake.*"

Harry didn't mean it to be condescending, but he wouldn't have said it if I were a man. I set my jaw, gripped my weapon in both hands with my elbows bent and the barrel pointing skyward, and crept into the alley.

The decaying garbage odor got worse with every step, so bad I could taste it in the back of my throat. I moved slowly, letting my eyes sweep left and right, looking for any place Bald Guy could hide. I came up to a parked car, checked under it, behind it.

"*Jesus, the stink is making my eyes water,*" Harry said. "*It smells like some fat guys with BO ate bad cheese and took a group shit on a rotting corpse.*"

Harry wore so much Brut aftershave I was surprised he could smell anything.

"You're a poet, McGlade."

"*Why? Did I rhyme something?*"

I stuck my head into a shadowy doorway, didn't find Bald Guy, and went deeper into the alley.

13

Then I heard the scream.

It came from ahead of me. A man's voice, with a hollow quality to it.

Something horrible was happening to Bald Guy.

My whole body became gooseflesh. I just joined Vice two weeks ago. Even though I was still a patrol officer and made the same pay, I jumped at the chance to wear plainclothes and ditch the standard uniform. But plainclothes turned out to be hooker-wear, and I felt especially vulnerable without my dress blues on. It wasn't easy being tough when you were wearing a micro-mini.

Another scream ripped through the alley. The little girl in me, the one who still woke up scared during thunderstorms, wanted to turn around and run.

But if I gave in to my fear, Harry would mention it in the arrest report. Then it would be back to riding patrol and answering radio calls, where I got even less respect.

I forced myself to move forward. Now my gun was pointing in front of me, toward the direction of the sound. The Beretta was double action, and protocol dictated it stayed uncocked. The harder pull meant fewer accidental shootings. Theoretically, at least. My finger was so tight on the trigger that a strong breeze would have caused me to fire.

"You see him?" Harry asked. I heard him in my earpiece, but I also heard him in the alley, somewhere ahead.

"Not yet."

"Maybe he's screaming because he can't stand the smell."

I didn't think that was the case. I'd heard my share of screams on the Job. Screams of joy. Screams of sorrow. Screams of pain.

This was a scream of terror.

A clanging sound, only a few yards away from me. A Dumpster. I held my breath, heard whimpering coming from inside.

"He's in a Dumpster," I told Harry.

"Probably sitting in a big pile of rats."

I approached quickly. It was dark, but I could see the Dumpster lid was open.

"This is the police!" I shouted, hoping my voice didn't quaver. "Raise your hands up where I can see them!"

Bald Guy complied. But there was something wrong. Rather than two hands, I counted three.

I moved closer and realized the third hand wasn't his. It belonged to a woman.

And it wasn't attached to the rest of her. Bald Guy was holding it, the look on his face pure horror.

I felt someone touch my shoulder and jumped back. It was Harry.

"Looks like he got you a birthday present, Jackie. Quite a handy guy."

My stomach seized up, and then I bent over and vomited, soaking my broken shoes and getting it caught in the fake curls hanging in front of my face. When I heaved for the final time, the transmitter popped free of my bustier and plonked into the puddle of puke.

"Happy twenty-ninth," Harry said.

Present day
2010, August 10

I flipped over onto my left side, my shoulders burning, my fingers beginning to go numb from the restricted blood flow. I closed my eyes and tried to relax my muscles. A cramp right now would be torture.

This new view didn't offer any revelations. I still couldn't see anything, still couldn't hear anything other than the hum of some machine. I stretched out my bound legs, seeking anything other than empty space, and my bare toes touched something.

Something flat, and metal. Cool, smooth, it made an empty sound, like tapping on a Dumpster. I kicked harder, feeling it vibrate, realizing it was a wall.

This wasn't a garage. It was a storage locker. Probably one of those self-storage spaces that people rented out.

And all at once I knew who had me. And I knew what he wanted to do with me.

My death wasn't going to be the worst of it. Death, when it came, would be a mercy.

I flexed my knees and kicked them against the corrugated aluminum wall as hard as I could, hoping someone would hear me.

Knowing no one would. Knowing what would come next.

Twenty-five years ago
1985, October 15

Sergeant Rostenkowski walked into the classroom and cleared his throat, getting everyone's attention. He was old—probably close to fifty—thick, with hands like two-by-fours, the knuckles covered with curly, gray hair. When he spoke, it was with utmost authority, and all of us took notes. Standing next to him was a short man in an ill-fitting suit whom we'd never seen before.

"Our guest speaker today is Dr. Malcolm Horner," the sergeant boomed, "a clinical psychiatrist from the University of Chicago."

Harry McGlade raised his hand and began talking without being called on. "Doc, I've been having these dreams where I'm trying to throw a spear at a giant pink pretzel, but every time I throw it my spear bends in half."

Everyone in class laughed, except for me. I nudged my one-piece chair and desk away from Harry and silently pitied the poor sap who got stuck being his partner after graduating from the police academy.

Dr. Horner smiled politely. "Your problem, Cadet, is firmly rooted in the fact that you have to be the center of attention, probably because your parents didn't love you enough."

Harry's grin fell away, but mine blossomed.

"My mom may not have loved me," Harry said, "but the last time I saw your mom, which was yesterday—"

"Can it, McGlade." Rostenkowski shot out one of his *cut the bullshit* looks, and Harry clammed up. "Now, please welcome Dr. Horner to our class."

The fifty or so cadets offered the psychiatrist a weak round of applause. It was close to dinner time, we'd been running drills all day, and I figured everyone was as hungry, exhausted, and brain dead as I was. While I was sure Dr. Horner would be tremendously enlightening (baloney, because during four weeks at the police academy the speakers had ranged from bland to downright awful), now wasn't a good time to absorb a lecture. But like any good student, I dutifully opened my notebook to a blank page and jammed a pen between my fingers.

"Gentlemen...and ladies," Dr. Horner acknowledged me, the only woman in the room. "Today I'm going to talk about evil."

My interest was piqued. In the nonstop lectures I'd been forced to endure about the criminal mind, the word *evil* hadn't been used before. We'd had terms like *socioeconomic factors* and *biological positivism* and *differential association* hammered into our heads, but nothing on evil.

This prompted a predictable outburst from Harry. "I just joined so I could catch bad guys."

While being a law enforcement officer had as much to do with how and why criminals became criminals as it did with how to catch them, part of me was with Harry on this issue.

While poverty, upbringing, and genetics all contributed to illegal behavior, I was more interested in stopping it than understanding it.

But evil? That was for philosophy class, not psychology. I thought about mentioning that, but someone in the front row beat me to the punch.

"We've been told evil doesn't exist. Last week, your colleague, Dr. Habersham, lectured that morality had no place in law enforcement. We're supposed to enforce the law, not judge right and wrong."

"I'm surprised you stayed awake long enough during Dr. Habersham's lecture to absorb that tidbit."

Laughter broke out. I was starting to like this guy.

"Indeed," he continued, "some schools of philosophy dictate that morality changes according to society. For example, in ancient Rome it was considered acceptable to throw people to the lions. A little over a hundred years ago, our country bought and sold human beings. Forty years ago, Germany endorsed genocide, something still common in modern times. For a recent example look at Cambodia and the killing fields, where more than two hundred thousand people were forced to dig their own graves before being beaten to death with ax handles because their executioners wanted to save on ammunition."

I looked around. No one was fidgeting or sleeping. Even Harry seemed to be paying attention.

"If we're going to discuss evil," Dr. Horner went on, "first we must decide whether evil is defined as an act, or as a trait. Let's do a thought experiment. An innocent, let's say a child, is murdered. By a show of hands, is this an evil act?"

Almost every hand went up. I kept mine on my desk. Dr. Horner met my eyes, pointed at me.

"Your hand didn't go up. Can you tell us why, Miss...?"

"Streng," I said. "Jacqueline Streng. There might be altru-istic intentions for the malice aforethought and..." my mind groped for the Latin term we recently learned, *"mens rea."*

Dr. Horner smiled. "I see you've been studying hard, Miss Streng, but please cut the jargon and give me an example when murdering a child isn't evil."

"What if it's a child dying of cancer, and in terrible pain? A parent, or someone else who loves the child, might attempt murder to end the suffering."

"Excellent, Miss Streng. Mercy killing, by law, meets the requirements for murder. The act of committing the crime, *actus reus*, and the willful intent to commit the crime, *mens rea*, is indeed malice aforethought, and according to the present law, that parent is a murderer. In this scenario, how many of you think the act is evil?"

No one raised their hand.

"But earlier, almost every hand was up. If the act itself isn't evil, what is?"

Someone said, "Motive."

"Ah." Dr. Horner nodded. "Now we're getting some-where. A parent's decision to murder is based on ending a child's agony. A noble, unselfish motive. Now let me show you a motive that's a bit more selfish. Lights, please."

Rostenkowski killed the lights, and Dr. Horner positioned himself behind a slide projector. He switched it on, and an image threw itself up on the movie screen on the far wall.

Someone coughed—an attempt to cover up a gag. I forced myself to look even though I had to hold my breath to do so. The temperature in the room seemed to drop ten degrees.

"This victim has never been identified. The missing fin-gers and missing teeth have made it impossible to trace who she is. They were removed while she was still alive. The mutilation here—"

Dr. Horner used a pointer and tapped the screen, touching the victim's pelvis.

"—was caused by a sharp instrument, a filet knife, or perhaps a scalpel. The victim was forced to eat these parts of herself. This white powder is salt, rubbed into the wounds. The burns here, here, here, and here were the result of a superheated flame. Possibly a blowtorch."

Dr. Horner turned away from the slide and stood in front of the screen, the ghastly image projected on his face and body.

"The autopsy determined, based on how some of the wounds had had time to heal, that she'd been tortured for at least twenty-four hours. We have no suspects, but some of the atrocities committed upon her have been seen in other, similar murders. The perpetrator has been dubbed *Unknown Subject K* by the FBI. We've taken to calling him Mr. K for short. Lights please, Sergeant."

The overhead fluorescent light flickered on. It reduced the brightness of the slide, but not enough. Details could still be seen.

"Now I present to you my earlier question. By a show of hands, who believes Mr. K is evil?"

Every hand went up but mine. Dr. Horner focused on me.

"Surely you don't believe this is a mercy killing, Miss Streng."

Titters from the peanut gallery.

"No. Of course not."

"So why didn't you raise your hand?"

"I don't know enough about the case."

Dr. Horner folded his arms across his chest. "What more do you need to know?"

22

"Was she raped?"

"Aw, come on!" Harry, naturally. "She was tortured for an entire day! What does it matter if she was raped, too?"

"Rape is a crime of violence," I stated, "but rapists tend to enjoy the act."

Dr. Horner tilted his head. "Sexual assault is unverified. Those parts of her were cut away. No semen was found."

"Was this the crime scene?" I asked. "Or was she dumped there?"

"We believe the apartment where she was discovered was where the crime was committed."

"Were there condoms found in the apartment? Condom wrappers?"

"No."

"Was it her apartment?"

"No. The room was supposed to be unoccupied."

"Were there neighbors?"

Dr. Horner offered a small smile. "Yes, on either side."

"No one heard her screams?"

"No. The same thing that allowed Mr. K to pry out her teeth also kept her from making any sound. A ball gag, holding her mouth open. Sold in sex shops across town and in the backs of pornographic magazines worldwide."

"Did he use ball gags on his other alleged victims?"

"Let's stick with this one. What is your reasoning that Mr. K might not be evil? His objective was obviously to cause pain and death."

I tapped my eraser against my desk. "But what was his motive? Did he do this because he knew the victim and hated her? Is he a sexual predator, a lust killer, who derived pleasure from his acts? Or was this murder dispassionate? Maybe someone paid him to commit these acts, but he had no feelings about it one way or the other."

"You're going to make an excellent police officer, Miss Streng," Dr. Horner said. "And I agree with you completely. Mr. K's intent was to murder in a ghastly fashion, but his motive might have been personal, sexual, or even financial. But the question is, which is the most evil?"

Dr. Horner stepped closer to me, so the victim's face projected onto his own.

"If you were at Mr. K's mercy, Miss Streng, would you prefer him to be a sexual sadist who delighted in your agony, or a cold-blooded mercenary who dispassionately inflicted these tortures because he was just following orders?"

Present day
2010, August 10

I flexed my fingers, my bound hands becoming dangerously numb. The ball gag felt enormous in my mouth. My heart was beating so fast I felt close to fainting.

I closed my eyes, forcing myself to concentrate. I'd been following the Mr. K case for more than twenty-five years. It was both my hobby and my white whale.

We'd crossed paths before. I'd logged in a lot of hours trying to catch him. A staggering one hundred and eighteen homicides had been attributed to the enigmatic killer.

Killer. Mr. Killer. That's the label the FBI attributed to him when they found a *"MR. K"* written in marker on a ball gag found at one of his scenes.

His victims seemingly had nothing in common. They were spread out across the nation, both men and women, ranging in age from seventeen to sixty-eight, encompassing many different races, religions, backgrounds, and histories.

The murder methods also varied wildly. Victims had been shot, stabbed, burned, broken, sliced, beaten, smashed, drowned, dismembered, and worse. The only thing that tied these unsolveds together were Mr. K's signatures: ball gags, salt in the wounds, and assorted, specific kinds of torture.

I wanted this guy. Wanted him bad. Unfortunately, hard evidence had always eluded me.

Ironic that I might have hard evidence very soon, but it would come at a very high cost.

I pushed away thoughts of death, concentrating on the here and now. I'd been awake long enough for my eyes to adjust, but it was still pitch black. Storage facilities usually had some kind of light, both in the units themselves and outside in the hallway. Since barely a sliver of light penetrated through any cracks, I assumed Mr. K either taped or filled in every corner of this space.

Total blackness was disorienting, making it impossible to focus on anything. But I was able to scoot toward the concrete block my legs were tethered to. I sat up, pushed myself backward against it, and explored the surface with my tingling fingers.

Too big and heavy to move. But it was square-shaped. While the edges weren't exactly sharp, the concrete was unfinished, rough. Was it enough to cut through the nylon cord securing my wrists?

Only one way to find out. I flexed my arms, sawing my binding against the stone's corner. I couldn't see my progress, and might not have even been making any, but I had excellent motivation to try.

I'd seen Mr. K's work up close and personal. And I knew what happened to the people he left in storage lockers.

Three years ago
2007, August 8

"You got anything to eat?" My partner, Detective First Class Herb Benedict, was rooting through my glove compartment.

Two blocks ahead, the man we'd been following turned his black Cadillac DTS onto Fullerton. I gave it a little gas and continued pursuit.

"Jack? Food? I'm starving here."

Herb was as far from starving as I was from dating George Clooney. He had to be close to the three hundred pound mark. Herb, not George.

"I think there's a box of bran flakes in the back seat somewhere."

Herb shifted his bulk around, making my Nova bounce on what little shocks it had left. After some grunting, and several glistening sweat beads popping out on his forehead, he found his prize.

"Got it." Herb cradled the cereal box in his hands like it was a kitten. Then he frowned. "They're bran flakes."

"That's what I said they were."

"Where's the milk?"

"No milk."

"You eat them dry?"

I sighed. "No. I eat them with milk. They fell out of my grocery bag, and I keep forgetting to bring them into the house."

"What am I supposed to do with these?"

"I have no idea. You asked if I had any food. I gave you what I had."

Herb made a face. The Cadillac pulled over to the curb, a few hundred yards ahead of us, next to a warehouse boasting the sign "U-Store-It." I parked alongside a fire hydrant and picked up the binoculars.

"Couldn't you have at least bought raisin bran?" Herb asked.

"I could have. But I didn't."

"Who doesn't like raisin bran?"

"My mother. They're for her."

Herb frowned. I peeked through the lenses and watched our person of interest exit his vehicle while Herb opened up the box.

"You're kidding me," I said, glancing at my partner.

"I gotta eat something. Look at me." He patted his protruding belly. "I'm wasting away to nothing."

Herb looked like he'd just eaten Santa Claus.

"We've got the rest of the day ahead of us," I told him. "I don't know if I want to spend it with you after you eat a box of bran."

"I just want a few nibbles."

My junior partner tore into the bag. I studied the surroundings. It wasn't a good part of town. Industrial mostly, a few overgrown, fenced-in lots, some abandoned factories. Certainly not a place where a man driving a new Cadillac would hang out.

"What's he doing?" Herb asked, his voice muffled by a mouthful of cereal.

"He's walking over to a self-storage building."

"Is he holding any milk? Because damn, this is dry."

"He's empty-handed." I played with the focus. "Jacket is swinging funny on his left side. He's packing."

"Maybe he's going to put it in storage." Herb cleared his throat. "You got anything to drink? These flakes sucked up all my saliva. It's like eating dust."

"I might have a bottle of water left. Check between your feet."

Herb rocked forward, trying to reach the floor. He failed. He tried again, bending even further, and then began to cough, spitting bran flakes all over my dashboard.

"Sorry," he mumbled.

I winced at the mess Herb had made. He tried once more for the water, stretching and straining, his face turning red with effort, and snatched the bottle. Herb held up his prize, triumphant. Then he frowned. "This is empty."

"He went in." I lowered the binocs. "Now we have a choice. We can wait for him to come out, then bust him, or surprise him inside and bust him."

"I vote for waiting," Herb said. "Less work. And if he's going in for something, maybe he'll come out with it."

We waited. Herb did a half-assed job wiping the bran off the dash, then sucked down the remaining five drops of water at the bottom of my bottle.

"I had a weird dream last night," Herb said.

"Speaking of non sequiturs."

"You want to hear it or not?"

"Is this the one where you're a caveman and everyone has a bigger spear than you?"

Herb raised an eyebrow. "What the hell are you talking about?"

"I remember someone saying something like that once. Thought it was you."

"It wasn't. My spear is above average size, not that it's any of your business. My dream was about lawn gnomes."

"Lawn gnomes."

"Yeah. A bunch of lawn gnomes."

"What were they doing?"

"Nothing. Just standing there, looking gnomish."

I pondered this for a moment. "And this is interesting because?"

"I dunno," my partner said. "You think it means anything?"

"Dreams don't mean anything at all, Herb. You know I don't buy into that stuff."

"You do lack a certain spirituality."

I checked through the binoculars again. Our person of interest hadn't returned. "I believe in facts, not superstition."

"How about chance? Coincidence? Fate?"

"Fate is a future you didn't work hard enough to change." I read that on a blog somewhere and liked it.

"Come on, Jack. Weird things happen all the time. Unexplainable, cyclical things."

"Such as?"

"How about when you hear a new word, then a few days later you hear it again?"

"Give me an example."

"The other day, on TV, someone said the word *lugubrious*. It means mournful."

"I know what it means," I said.

"Really? I had to look it up. Anyway, two days later, I'm at the butcher shop, and guess what word he uses?"

"Bacon?"

"*Lugubrious.* Things like that get me thinking. It's like hitting your finger with a hammer, and then ten years later, hitting it again in the exact same place. You could have hit any other finger, or any other spot. But it was right smack-dab on the previous injury. What does that tell you?"

"That you shouldn't be using a hammer."

Herb shook his head. "I think that maybe, just maybe, there is some sort of grand scheme to everything."

"You mean God?"

"I mean maybe the universe has a sense of irony."

I didn't agree, but I couldn't completely disregard the comment either. Sometimes things did happen that could make you scratch your head.

"Think this guy might really be Mr. K?" I asked.

"Personally, I think Mr. K is an urban legend, started by one Dr. Horner to scare rookies and prove his BS about good and evil."

I recalled that police academy lecture, and probably still had the notes from it.

"Over a hundred unsolved homicides, the only links being torture and ball gags," I said.

"Why do they have to be connected? Because the Feebies say so?"

"You know my feelings about the Feds, Herb. But I've looked at these cases. The murder methods vary wildly, but

31

there's something about them that seems similar. Call it, I dunno, a *tone*."

"Not every murderer is a serial killer, Jack."

He was right. But I seemed to wind up dealing with more than my fair share.

Herb put his hand in the bran box again, going for seconds.

"If you spit bran in my car again, I'm firing you."

"Like it's my fault you don't have any milk. I almost choked to death. Horrible way to die." I endured more munching sounds. "Didn't Mr. K choke his last victim?"

"Stuffed the guy's junk down his own throat."

"While it was still attached?"

"Severed first."

"Would have been more impressive if it was still attached." Herb ate more bran. "Jesus, this is dry. It's like eating sand, but with less flavor."

Herb put another handful into his mouth.

Finally I said, "I think we should go in."

"I thought waiting for him was easier. Then we can grab him with whatever he brings out."

"But if we get him now, then we can check out his storage space ourselves. Probable cause, no warrant needed."

"I'm for staying in the car," Herb said. "It's hot out, and my feet hurt."

He had a point. It was hot. And chances were high the warehouse wasn't air-conditioned.

"Flip a coin?" I asked.

He shrugged. "Okay."

I checked my purse but as expected didn't find any change. I got rid of it whenever possible, not wanting to jingle when I walked. It used to annoy my ex-husband, Alan. I didn't keep him, but I kept the habit.

"Got any coins?" I asked Herb.

"No. Vending machines are my nemesis."

"I thought your shoelaces were your nemesis."

Herb got a full aerobic workout whenever he tried to tie his shoes.

"A cop of my longevity makes many enemies throughout his career."

"Check the ashtray."

Herb checked while I took another look through the binocs. Nothing happening. I picked up the radio handset and called Dispatch, requesting possible backup.

My partner found something in the ashtray, but rather than flip it and call it, he popped it into his mouth.

"Did you just eat a dime?" I asked.

"Hell no. It was a mint." He made a face. "I think."

I tried to recall the last time I had mints in the car. It had been years. No, a decade, at least.

"It was a dime," Herb said, sticking out his tongue. "I was fooled by the fuzz."

I decided not to ask Herb why he would eat anything covered in fuzz. The radio crackled. Car 917 responded, saying they were en route. Approximate arrival in two minutes.

I made the executive decision. "We're going in."

"What happened to flipping a coin?"

"You ate the coin."

"How about rock, paper, scissors?"

"You really don't want to get out of the car, do you?"

Herb frowned. "What do we know about the guy? Sure, he's got possible criminal associations and an expensive condo, but he hasn't even gotten so much as a parking ticket, for chrissakes. His record is squeaky clean."

"He's carrying a gun."

"Did you see a gun? Or just a bulge in his jacket? Maybe he was carrying an iPod, or a can of pop, or a magazine."

"Or a lawn gnome."

"Did you see a red, pointy hat? That would be eerie."

"It was a gun," I said.

"I'm just trying to protect you from a false arrest lawsuit."

"God, you're lazy."

"I prefer the term *cautiously inactive.*"

"Okay. Rock, paper, scissors. One, two, three..."

I held out a flat palm: paper. Herb had a fist. Rock.

"Paper covers rock," I said. "We go in."

"Wait, it's two out of three. It's always two out of three."

I sighed. "Okay. One, two, three..."

I held out paper again. Herb held out a single, chubby finger.

"What the hell is that?"

"That's a hot dog."

"A hot dog?"

"I'm starving. I can't get my mind off of food."

"Again," I said. "No hot dogs this time. One, two, three..."

I made a rock. Herb, paper.

"I win," he said.

"You sure that's paper, not a sirloin steak?"

"Mmm. Steak. Stop teasing me."

"One more time. One, two, three..."

I held out scissors. So did Herb.

"My scissors are bigger," he said. "I win."

I said, "One, two, three..."

I had a rock. Herb stuck with scissors. I won.

"We're going in."

I hit the gas, driving the two blocks' distance in about eight seconds, parking in front of the Cadillac. Then I dug my Colt out of my purse, checked the cylinder, and got out of my car. A moment later, Herb rocked himself out of his seat and onto the sidewalk.

"Be pretty funny if this was Mr. K, wouldn't it?" he said.

"It would be the perfect gift to myself."

"Oh, yeah." Herb nodded, his three chins wiggling. "Your birthday is in a few days. You don't have much luck with birthdays. Remember Classy Companions?"

My lips pressed together, forming a tight line. "I remember."

Herb must have noted my expression. "Sorry, Jack. Didn't know that was still a sore spot. I'm sure this birthday will turn out a lot better."

"Can't be any worse than the last twenty."

Herb checked the clip on his Sig. "Okay. Let's go do it."

"Now? Backup will be here in a minute."

"I bet you dinner the only thing he's got in his jacket is a magazine."

I nodded at Herb. "You're on."

We headed for the entrance, and I was feeling pretty optimistic. Maybe I'd finally have a decent birthday for a change. My fiancé was out of town on business, but closing a hundred unsolved homicides was definitely the way I wanted to spend my forty-seventh.

Besides, I was more than a little curious about what he was keeping in that storage locker.

Present day

2010, August 10

The man known as Mr. K holds up the iPhone and stares at the soft, green image on the touch screen. Jack Daniels rubs her wrists against the concrete anchor, her eyes wide and glowing in the night vision camera.

Her expression is one he recognizes well.

Fear. She's afraid.

And she has good reason to be.

Their little dance has been going on for a long time. For the better part of both their careers. The ex-cop had gotten closer than anyone else ever had.

He taps the screen, bringing up the control dial. Twirling his finger, he adjusts the camera angle and zooms in to Jack's hands.

She's bleeding. The rope and the concrete are causing abrasions on her wrists. It will sting like crazy because he dusted the rope in salt before tying her up.

That's only the first taste, Jack. There will be more pain to come. Much more.

Mr. K sets the iPhone up on a stand, so the image faces him. Then he picks the filet knife off the table.

It's a tool he's used on countless occasions, bought at a live bait store on Chicago's South Side almost three decades ago. He's sharpened it so many times, the blade is less than a centimeter wide. It looks more like an ice pick than a knife.

Mr. K tests the blade's sharpness, touching it lightly to the back of his thumbnail. He's able to draw a line across the lunula—the bottom of the nail—with barely any pressure. The knife is honed to a razor's edge, so he puts it in its sheath and sets it aside.

Next he checks the propane torch. After a quick shake, he determines the handheld tank to be half full. That's not enough fuel for what he has planned, so he unscrews the pencil-flame top from the canister and attaches it to a fresh tank.

The final tool on his workbench is a two-pound ball-peen hammer with a plastic composite shank extending from the stainless steel head down through the handle. This requires no fine tuning, so he lets it be.

Over the years, he's used just about every device imaginable to inflict pain. He had a phase where he preferred power tools. A phase where he only used his gloved hands. For a two-year stretch, every murder he committed was done with a car jack; with wire ties it could be used to easily detach joints from sockets.

But after a lifetime of trial and error, he decided the simplest ways were ultimately the best. Cutting. Burning. Breaking. Everything beyond that was just showing off.

He glances at his iPhone again. Jack's eyes are squeezed shut, her jaw muscles clenching down on the ball gag.

Think that hurts, Lieutenant? Just wait until tonight.

Because tonight, Mr. K *will* show off.

Twenty-one years ago
1989, August 16

The Cook County Morgue smelled like a butcher shop from Dante's seventh circle of hell.

Underneath the acrid stench of bleach and spray disinfectant, there was the unmistakable odor of meat. But it was meat on the verge of going bad—the beginning stages of rot that all the chemicals in the world couldn't completely mask.

I was standing in one of the autopsy rooms, staring down at the headless corpse of a naked Caucasian woman—the one we'd discovered in the Dumpster while chasing that bald john the night before. Her arms and legs were severed, but Medical Examiner Phil Blasky—a balding man with an egg-shaped head—had placed them in the appropriate spots along her torso.

I wondered if they would be sewn back on before burial, or if it didn't matter, since she didn't have a head.

I'd traded my hooker outfit for plainclothes—a gray, off-the-rack pantsuit I bought at Sears. It was too loose in the butt and too tight in the chest, and with my hair pulled back

I looked somewhat like an effeminate man. Especially since I'd forsaken makeup, having had enough of the gunk caked on me yesterday. In the car ride over to the morgue, I spent five solid minutes trying to convince my partner, Harry McGlade, that I wasn't a lesbian.

Harry nudged me with his elbow, then pointed to the dead woman's chest.

"Look how perky they are, even in death. Think they're even paid for yet?"

The corpse's implants stuck out like two torpedoes. Except for their color—a very pale blue—they looked like they'd popped right out of the pages of *Playboy*.

"Maybe you should have that done," Harry said. "You're sort of lacking in that department, Jackie."

"You forgot to take your pill today, Harry."

"My pill?"

"Your *shut the fuck up* pill."

"You're funny."

"And you're seven kinds of stupid. You ever want to make detective?"

Harry shrugged.

"Well, I do," I said through my teeth as Blasky came back into the room. "So try to act like a cop."

Harry saluted me. "Yes, sir."

Asshole. I still couldn't believe I got stuck with him as a partner.

Blasky stood across the autopsy table from us. He nodded at me. Unlike the old boys' network back at the district house, Blasky treated me like a cop, not like a girl or a pretender to the throne.

"Do you know the cause of death?" I asked.

"I'm not a doctor," Harry said, "but I'd put my money on the severed head and limbs."

Blasky smiled condescendingly at Harry. "Then you'd lose your money," Blasky said, his voice deep and commanding, not far off from Darth Vader's. "The amputations were post-mortem. CAT scan shows she died from internal hemorrhaging. Several major organs were pierced."

"How?" Harry folded his arms across his chest. "There are no stab wounds at all."

I was wondering the same thing, but then I noticed a trickle of blood seeping out between the woman's legs.

"A sharpened broomstick," I said.

Blasky raised an eyebrow. "That's my guess as well. We'll know for sure when I open her up. Why didn't you think it was a sword? Or a poker?"

"Those would have damaged her labia."

"What?" McGlade asked. "You mean someone stuck a... oh, shit...that's *sick*."

"Have you swabbed for semen?" I asked.

"Yes. Negative."

That didn't rule out rape. Perp could have used a condom. The cause of death made this an obvious sex murder.

"Defense marks?" I asked.

The medical examiner shook his head. "No. No ligature marks either. I'm betting the blood work shows drugs."

After discovering the body in the Dumpster last night, I'd stayed and watched the crime scene team do their work. They'd dusted for prints on the body and come up negative. They'd also scraped under the fingernails in the hope the victim scratched her killer and picked up some of his skin cells or blood. Chicago had adopted the new DNA profiling technique begun in England, and it could directly link a perp to a crime by determining a genetic match.

But if the victim were drugged to the point where she didn't even need to be tied up while she was being assaulted, chances weren't high there would be DNA evidence.

I put my hand in front of my face to stifle a yawn. After watching the crime scene guys do their thing, I'd had to write my report of the murder, as well as my report for arresting the john who hopped into the Dumpster after asking me to manipulate his prostate. As a result, I slept a total of two hours, and that was mostly tossing and turning. I'd been struggling with insomnia since graduating the police academy, but I was pretty sure it was a transitory thing.

At least, I hoped it was.

The door to the autopsy room opened, and two men walked in. Both were thin, both were older than McGlade and I. One was dressed like me—a cheap suit, barely concealing the shoulder holster. He had a thick, wide mustache that looked a lot like Teddy Roosevelt's. I don't think he could have appeared more like a stereotypical Homicide detective if he tried.

The other wore a gray suit that fit like it was made just for him and probably cost more than I earned in a month. He obviously wasn't a cop, and he was kind of cute, in a strong-jawed male-model sort of way.

The cop eyed Harry and me, then held out his hand.

"Detective Herb Benedict, Homicide. Call me Herb."

His grip was warm and confident.

"Officer Jacqueline Streng. Jacqueline is fine." I hated when Harry called me *Jackie*.

"Who's the suit?" Harry asked.

The good-looking man answered, "Armani."

"Pleased to meet you, Mr. Armani," I said, extending my hand.

The man's eyes twinkled. "The suit is made by a designer named Giorgio Armani. My name is Shell Compton."

His grip was also warm and confident, but it lingered longer than Herb's.

"This one of your whores, Shelly?" Harry asked, jerking a thumb at the corpse.

Shell's face got hard, and he took his hand back and stared at McGlade. "None of the ladies who work with me are whores. They're escorts, and what they chose to do with their clients is their business and perfectly legal."

"Huh," Harry said. "Never met a self-righteous pimp before."

"Is he your partner?" Shell asked me.

I nodded.

Shell tilted his head to the side and whispered, so only I heard him. "I'm so sorry."

Then we all turned our attention to the body. I watched Shell's eyes, watched his look of shock turn to sadness when he noticed the tattoo on the corpse's ankle.

"That's Linda," he said, shoulders sagging.

"You're sure?" Herb asked.

"Tattoo on her ankle. Mole on her collarbone." He turned away, glassy-eyed.

Herb flipped open a handheld notepad. "You reported Linda Candell missing yesterday. She'd been gone for forty-eight hours prior to that."

Shell nodded. "Linda wasn't flighty. She didn't just disappear, and she'd never miss a date with a client. I tried to file a police report after she missed her first appointment, but I was told I had to wait two days." He looked at the ME. "When did she die?"

Blasky clucked his tongue. "Hard to say. When I took her core temperature, it was seventy degrees. In that heat, in that dumpster, it should have been at least a hundred. I think, after she was murdered, the killer put her on ice. Not a freezer—there aren't freezer burns. But someplace cold."

I felt a shiver crawl up my backbone. Being horribly murdered was bad enough. Getting stuck in a refrigerator afterward, like meat, was one of the worst things I'd ever heard.

Shell must not have cared for the idea either. He excused himself and hurried out of the room. Herb tucked his notebook into his breast pocket and turned to me.

"How long have you been doing Vice stings, Jacqueline?"

"Yesterday was my sixth night."

"Do you think you can do an undercover operation for longer than a night? Say, a week or two?"

I felt my pulse quicken, wondering if this would be my opportunity to finally work Homicide. Goodbye spandex skirts and slutty high heels. Hello respect and commendation.

"This is the third body in six weeks," Herb continued. "Same MO. All escorts. Two of them worked for Shell."

"He's gotta be the killer," Harry said. "I don't trust guys who wear nice clothes."

Both Herb and I ignored him. "You're thinking I pose as an escort," I said.

Herb nodded. "I've already talked to my captain. You'd be placed in Shell's operation, working full time. He's already agreed. We think it might be someone close to his business, maybe a client or a competitor. You wouldn't have to do anything sexual. Shell was telling the truth; his escort service is simply an escort service, not a prostitution ring. You'd wear a wire the whole time, be under full surveillance—"

"I'll do it," I said, interrupting him.

Herb stared at me. He had a kind face, but his gaze was hard. "Wasn't too long ago I was a uniform, eager to get into plainclothes. But this is serious, Jacqueline. The man doing this is a monster."

I gave him a hard stare right back. "I'm in. This is why I became a cop."

We held the intensity for a few seconds in silence, then Herb grinned. "Great," he said, chuckling.

Was he mocking me? I folded my arms across my chest. "Is something funny, Detective?"

Herb shook his head. "Not at all. I just have this feeling we're going to work well together."

Present day
2010, August 10

I began to cry. My eyes stung like I'd been hit with mace. But the real sting was in my wrists.

The bastard had dipped the rope around my arms in salt.

As I sawed away at the edge of the concrete, determined to break the rope, it eventually began to rub my skin raw. The pain was quite extraordinary for such a superficial wound. I put it up alongside root canals and getting shot and breaking my leg.

Mr. K liked salt. It was a trademark of his, along with the ball gag.

I really have to get out of here.

I continued to work on the rope, tears streaming down my face, biting down on the rubber ball to help with the pain, trying not to think about Mr. K's other trademarks.

The ones I'd seen firsthand.

Three years ago
2007, August 8

I walked briskly to the storage facility, minding each step so I didn't scrape my Jimmy Choos. They weren't the most appropriate footwear for police work, but a long time ago a man taught me that more people remembered style than deeds, and that stuck. Even so, I tried to overcompensate with deeds in an effort to compete with my boundless style.

Herb waddled behind me, wheezing. I slowed my pace just a tad, letting him catch up, trying to remember what he used to be like when he was thin. Back in the day, Herb Benedict could run a hundred meters in thirteen seconds. Now it would take him two minutes. Seven minutes if he had to stop to tie his shoes. Eighteen minutes if there was a hot dog stand on the route.

Merle's U-Store-It was an ugly brown building, the dirty brick coated in graffiti so old even the taggers didn't think it worthwhile anymore. It was a few stories tall, probably a converted warehouse or factory from the days when Chicago was an industrial hub. The entrance was a single metal door with a sign next to it, proclaiming they were open six a.m. until midnight, seven days a week.

The door opened to a narrow hallway, a bare forty-watt bulb stuck in the ceiling, which made the grimy walls look even dingier. A few yards down was the obligatory manager/watchman, behind a protective barrier of bulletproof glass that bore a few divots. Black guy, short beard, scar on his nose. At the moment, all the watchman was watching was a portable television set up on his desk. He didn't even glance at us when we walked up, and I had to rap on the window to get his attention.

"New rental contracts are on the table," he droned. "If you forgot your key, I need two forms of ID, and there's a five-dollar charge."

He still hadn't looked at us.

"Police," I said, fishing my gold badge from the pocket of my Tignanello handbag and clinking it against the glass.

"Police still gotta pay the five bucks." He kept his eyes on the TV.

"We're here to arrest the man who just came in. Did you see him?"

"Didn't see nuthin'."

I looked around the cubbyhole he used as an office. No security system. No surveillance equipment. If he didn't see the guy, there was no way he'd know which storage unit he owned. This place was so low tech I was surprised the entrance had an electric lock.

"Buzz us in," I said, using my cop tone.

"Got a warrant?"

I considered saying yes. It was doubtful he'd turn away from the television to check. Instead I said, "I don't need a warrant. I'm arresting him for carrying a concealed weapon.

You want some guy with a gun running around your building?"

"Ain't my building. I just work here."

Now I understood the reason for the bulletproof glass. I'd known this guy for less than thirty seconds, and I was overcome with a fierce desire to shoot him.

"Let me see some ID, sir," I ordered.

Now he looked at me, his expression pained. "Why you got to hassle me, *offa-sir?*"

I was the one hassling him?

"Open the goddamn door, pinhead," Herb said.

The watchman buzzed us in. Incredible. I'd been on the force for over twenty years and outranked Herb, but because he was a man he automatically got more respect. So little had changed since I was a rookie.

The metal security door opened. I walked through and saw a lobby, which boasted a metal garbage can, a freight elevator, a door that said STAIRS, and corridors going left and right. Above the elevator were lights indicating three floors.

"Cover the exit and call me," I told Herb, digging my Bluetooth earpiece out of my purse and attaching it to the side of my head. "This may take a while."

I went into the stairwell, figuring I'd start on the third floor and work my way down. The storage units here had garage-style doors, secured with padlocks. Even if he was inside his unit with the door closed behind him, all I had to do was look for the missing lock and I'd know it was his.

The stairway smelled dusty, like old drywall. I listened for movement, heard nothing, then took the concrete steps two at a time, unbuttoning the strap over the Colt in my shoulder holster. My earpiece buzzed and I pressed the tiny button.

"They need to make these headsets bigger," Herb said. *"It's too small for my fingers."*

"Maybe you need to make your fingers smaller." I was on the second floor. I eased open the door and poked my head through, just to see if our man was around. He wasn't, so I continued up the stairs.

"If this really is Mr. K," Herb said, *"what's he storing here?"*

"Maybe his money."

One of the many persistent rumors circulating about the mysterious Mr. K was that he worked as a contract killer for the Outfit. With over a hundred unsolved murders attributed to him, perhaps he actually did need a storage locker to store all of his cash. Banks kept records of large deposits, and most of the mobsters I knew didn't pay by check.

If Mr. K *was* a hired gun, he was an iceman. I'd dealt with a few serial killers over the years, and their motives made a warped sort of sense; hurting and killing people was exciting to them. But I believed contract killers, and contract torturers, were a whole different breed. If evil really existed, did it manifest itself in psychopaths who enjoyed inflicting pain on others? Or was it a trait of otherwise normal people who committed atrocities for money, because they were just following orders? Which was worse, killing because you liked it? Or killing because you just didn't give a shit about humanity?

I stepped out of the stairwell onto the third floor, knowing I really didn't need an answer to that question. My job wasn't to psychoanalyze criminals. It was to catch them. And if our suspect was really Mr. K, it would be the high point of my career to put the bastard away.

The third floor hallway was empty in both directions, and I didn't see any open storage units. I walked slowly, looking at padlocks. Every door had either a lock, or a metal band that sealed the unrented units.

I turned the corner, then stopped. A few yards ahead, one of the doors to a storage unit was open about a foot and a half, some light pouring through the bottom.

"Third floor, unit 345," I whispered to Herb. "Ask the manager who it belongs to."

I listened to Herb ask, heard mild protestations and more talk of warrants, and then my partner used some very bad language and the manager became cooperative.

"*Cute,*" Herb said. "*It's rented under the name John Smith. Paid for the month, and the deposit, with cash. I'm looking at his rental agreement. Listed his place of residence as 2650 South California Avenue.*"

Cute was right. That was the address of the Criminal Courts Building, adjacent to Cook County Jail.

"Check on our backup. I'm approaching 345."

I dug out my Colt, its weigh reassuring, and approached the storage unit on the balls of my feet so my heels didn't click. This was one of the larger units, with an orange metal door that lifted overhead on rollers. It was three-quarters of the way closed, which meant it was open about eighteen inches. When I got within three feet I squatted down, checking to see if someone was standing inside. I didn't see legs, but toward the rear of the storage area I caught a shadow of movement.

I aimed my weapon at the door. "This is Lieutenant Daniels of the Chicago Police. I'm ordering the man in unit 345 to come out slowly, hands in the air. This is a direct command from a police officer."

I pressed my back against the door of an adjacent unit, out of the line of fire. Then I listened.

No response. No movement.

"I repeat, a Chicago police officer is giving you an order. If you don't come out right now, hands in the air, I will open fire."

I wasn't going to open fire. I could just picture the inquest and subsequent suspension and lawsuit if I shot someone through the door to a storage unit. But nine times out of ten, suspects usually followed my commands.

I waited. Apparently this was a one out of ten situation. Setting my jaw, I eased myself over to the door, getting down on one knee, looking under the space between it and the floor. Again I saw movement, near the rear.

Without hesitating, I gripped the underside of the door and jerked it, sending it upward on its rollers, extending my gun hand with my finger on the trigger, moving fast into the space, ready for anything.

But I wasn't ready for this. In twenty years on the force, this was the most horrible thing I'd ever seen.

"Jesus Christ," I whispered.

"Jack?" Herb said in my earpiece. He said some other things as well, but I didn't hear them because I was bent over, throwing up my breakfast all over my Jimmy Choos—something I hadn't done since I was a rookie working Vice.

When I recovered, I checked the hallway both left and right, sweeping the area even though the perp was obviously gone. The only thing the storage unit contained was the IV stand, an empty tripod, the machine, and the misshapen, naked, dead man with the slit throat.

Then the dead man opened his eyes. I couldn't hear his agonizing moan through the ball gag, but his pinched face spoke of unbearable pain.

I hurried to him, hitting the button on the infernal machine to stop the rotation even though I was potentially contaminating a crime scene. Then I pressed my hand to the gushing wound in the man's neck, even as he thrashed away from my touch.

"Herb! Call an ambulance! And cover the exit, our perp—"

"Holy shit."

I heard Herb twice, first in both ears and then in one. I turned and saw him standing there, jaw open, staring at me and the vic.

Herb did what I'd done. He turned and puked.

My mind seemed to both slow down and speed up at the same time. If Herb was up here, there was no one covering the exit. We needed to catch that son of a bitch. But we also needed to save this poor bastard, which meant calling an ambulance. And I couldn't take my hand off his neck, or off my gun, in case the perp came back.

"HERB!" I shouted with all I had. "AMBULANCE!"

He pulled it together, calling the paramedics on his radio, then calling backup to tell them to cover the car parked outside. Hot blood gushed through my fingers, down my arm.

"Backup's still a minute away," Herb said.

I thought about ordering him downstairs to try to head Mr. K off—because there was no doubt this was Mr. K—but I wouldn't send him after that maniac without backup.

"Cover the hallway," I said, tucking my gun into my holster and unbuckling the ball gag on the victim because he was blowing air through the hole in his neck.

As soon as the gag dropped free, he cried out in a voice that would haunt my nightmares forever.

"LET ME DIE! LET ME DIE!"

But I couldn't let him die, even though he eventually did. I kept pressure on his neck wound, trying not to look at him, trying not to cry, not even able to talk soothingly to him as his life mercifully slipped away.

Twenty-one years ago
1989, August 16

"What we're proposing," Herb said, the beer in front of him untouched, "is deeper undercover than you've ever been before."

We were in a local pub on Addison, sitting at a high, round table on high, round bar stools, squinting at each other in the low lighting and talking over the ten TVs showing local sports.

"We're thinking at least two weeks," Herb continued.

Harry snorted into his glass of Old Style, spraying foam across the table. "You not only want Jackie to pretend to be an escort, but to do it for more than a day or two? Gimme a break."

I steeled my eyes at McGlade, wondering what I'd done in a previous life to deserve him. Maybe I'd been Joseph Stalin, or some other genocidal maniac.

"I've been doing undercover stings for two weeks now, McGlade. I can handle it."

"You've been playing street whores, Jackie. All you need is a short skirt. Escorts are classy ladies. They dress nice. They talk nice. They look nice. You don't wear makeup, and when you do doll yourself up, you put on your eye shadow with a paint roller and look like Big Bird from *Sesame Street*. And your clothes? Was Montgomery Wards having a sale on suits in the teenage boys department?"

It was Sears, not Wards. But I wasn't about to give him any more ammo.

"We're done," Herb said. He was talking to Harry.

Harry raised his eyebrows. "Excuse me?"

"We want Jacqueline for this. Not you. I already cleared it. Go talk to your captain about reassignment."

Harry blinked. Then he blinked again. "But Jackie's my partner."

"*Was* your partner. For this case, she's my partner. Now I'll let you sit here and finish your beer, but keep your mouth shut. I'm sick of hearing it."

Harry got down off his bar stool, sticking out his chin. "I get it. You're grumpy because your wife doesn't give you any, and you didn't have time this morning to rub one out in the shower. So now you're pulling rank, getting your rocks off that way. Well, I've got better things to do than hang out in this dumb bar with you dumb people." He nodded at me. "Good night, Jackie."

Then he left our table, and sat down one table over.

"Was that guy dropped down the stairs as a baby?" Herb asked me.

"I think he was dropped down an escalator, and fell for three hours."

Herb smiled at me. I decided I liked him, in a big brother kind of way.

I also liked our drinking companion, Shell. But in a way that decidedly wasn't big brotherish. The guy I was dating, Alan, was a moody, artsy type, and his neuroses merged well with mine. Shell was polished and cocksure and easy to look at. The type of guy I secretly wanted to go out with in college, but who intimidated me with their charisma.

I was determined not to be intimidated this time. Even if it meant I had to sleep with him to get over it.

"So you think I can do this?" I was looking at Shell, not Herb.

Shell leaned over the table, his hands sliding forward so his knuckles brushed mine. "I do. I think you'll be perfect."

Herb drained half his beer, spilling a bit on his tie. "This isn't like streetwalker stings, Jacqueline. Your obnoxious partner is right. We don't know who's doing this to Shell's girls. Could be a client. Could be someone on the inside. Could be a stranger, stalking from the shadows. You'll need to live the part. It means rooming with the other girls, talking to them like you're one of them, actually *becoming* one of them. It means going out on dates."

"But I don't have to..."

"Make love to them?" Shell asked, offering a sly smile. "No. We're a legitimate escort service. A real estate broker needs arm candy for his high school reunion. Mortgage banker needs a date to his niece's wedding. Lonely widower doesn't want to eat out alone. That type of thing. It's all legitimate, and our clients are aware they aren't allowed to hit on the girls unless the girl makes the first move."

"How often does that happen?" I asked.

In the background, the bar broke out into cheers and applause.

"Some of our clients are rich, powerful men," Shell said. "Some are famous. Whatever two consenting adults decide to do privately has nothing to do with me or my business, and it's all off the clock."

"Can you do this, Jacqueline?" Herb said.

I stared at Shell. "Yes."

"You'd be living with the other girls. You might be away from home for a while."

I thought about my crappy Wrigleyville apartment. "Not a problem."

"If you have a pet, a cat—"

I shook my head. "I hate cats. I'd never own a cat."

"Do you have any objections to starting tomorrow?" Herb asked. "Your captain said Homicide can have you on loan for as long as we need you."

I struggled to suppress a giggle. Me? Working Homicide? That had only been my goal since joining the force.

"Tomorrow sounds fine," I said, keeping a straight face.

"Great!" Shell clasped my hands, in a way that was both formal yet intimate. "Welcome to Classy Companions."

"We'll get started in the morning," Herb said. "I can pick you up."

"I've got a car," I said. It was a Nova, only a few years old.

"Okay. Meet me at the station at eight a.m."

"Sounds good." I glanced at Shell. "What should I wear?"

"Something nice," he said.

"How nice are we talking, here?"

"I'll take care of that." He gave my hands an extra squeeze.

"I'll meet you both tomorrow," Herb said. "In the meantime, I've pulled the victims' files. I'd like you to take a look, see if you spot anything we missed. I'm anxious to hear your take on this."

Herb pulled some files from his briefcase. He stacked them onto the table, pushing them over to me. If he'd called me the most beautiful woman on the planet, it couldn't have flattered me more. My respect for Herb kept going up and up.

"I'll get started on these right away," I promised.

The waitress brought the bill to Herb, and he squinted at it, making a face.

"We didn't order thirty-two shots of tequila."

She smacked her gum and cocked out a hip. "Your friend did. The one who was sitting at the table next to you. He bought shots for everyone in the bar, but said for us to skip you guys because you were driving."

Shell smiled politely and took the bill. I looked around for Harry, but he'd wisely made a quick exit. Annoying as he was, the guy did have a certain lowbrow style.

"See you tomorrow," Herb said, standing up. "Partner."

He stuck out his hand. I shook it gladly. Herb nodded a goodbye to Shell, then left the restaurant.

"He's a good guy," Shell said, running his finger along the edge of his beer glass.

"Seems like it," I agreed.

"Has the metabolism of a hummingbird. Before we went to the morgue I watched him polish off three hot dogs with the works. I don't know where he puts it. The guy should weigh three hundred pounds."

I tried to imagine thin-as-a-rail Herb weighing that much, but just couldn't see it.

"So tell me," Shell said, leaning forward on the table so his knuckles brushed mine again, "what's a nice girl like you doing in a career like this?"

I'd been asked that before, but never like that. Most people wondered what was wrong with me for wanting to be a cop. When Shell asked me, I felt like my job impressed him.

"Mom was on the force," I said, leaning closer, letting our fingers meet. I liked it that Shell was confident enough to flirt with me, and wondered how far he would take it if I let him. "But she joined in the sixties. Women didn't climb the ranks, and we didn't get the due respect."

"Is that what you're looking for? Rank and respect?"

I answered without hesitation. "Yes."

"What rank are you shooting for?"

"I'm going to make lieutenant by the time I'm forty."

Shell ran his index finger over the back of my hand. "I'm sure you will."

I probably should have pulled away. But Shell was attractive, and saying all the right things, and I was feeling bold and a bit reckless. My so-called boyfriend, Alan, hadn't so much as called me on my birthday yesterday. That stung. Neither of us had said *I love you* yet, and even though he had a key to my place we'd never had the *we're exclusive* talk. So if I wound up doing anything with Shell I wouldn't be cheating.

But I wasn't going to do anything with Shell. At least, not at that moment. I'd only met the guy two hours ago. I considered myself liberated, but that didn't mean I was easy.

"So how about you?" I asked. "How did you wind up running an escort service?"

Shell's lips formed a small grin, and he glanced away, back to some long-ago memory. "I've always liked the finer things in life. Food, wine, fashion, cars, hotels." His eyes centered on mine. "Women."

The way he said it made me feel like I was, indeed, one of the finer things in life.

"A few years ago I was dating a dynamite woman," he continued. "Smart. Sassy. Beautiful. She was a model, but finding it increasingly difficult to find paying gigs. She told me she was considering becoming an escort to make ends meet, but was clueless about how to get started. I took it upon myself to help her. For my assistance, she gave me twenty percent of the escort money she earned. She also recommended I help some of her friends do the same thing. A business was born."

"When was the first murder?"

Shell's face clouded, and I was a little sorry I'd lapsed into cop mode. But I needed this information, and talking to someone who knew the victims would be more helpful than reading about them in police reports.

"A month ago," Shell said. "Her name was Nancy. Nancy Slusar. Like Linda, she'd been..." Shell swallowed, "...hacked to pieces."

"Did Nancy, Linda, or you have any enemies?"

"I gave Detective Benedict a short list. Three disgruntled clients. Several women I had to fire for inappropriate behavior. A guy who kept hanging around, wanting to date one of the girls."

"How about business competition? How do you get along with the other escort services?"

"The girls often sign up with more than one service, to maximize the amount of dates they get. We're mostly ambivalent about each other."

"Mostly?" I probed.

"There is one service—the Dodd Agency—who has aggressively tried to pursue some of my girls, wanting them exclusively. I had to retain a lawyer to get them to stop it. I believe they're Outfit owned and operated."

"Outfit?"

"You know. The mob."

I wished I'd had a notepad like Herb's to write this stuff down. Instead, I committed it to memory.

"So." Shell's tone changed, from sad and guarded to flirty once again. "Are you ready to go shopping?"

"Shopping?"

"For clothing. You have to look the part for your photo."

I had no idea where he was going with this. "What photo?"

"For your portfolio. Clients choose their dates based on a photo and a detailed bio. So we need to go shopping, get you something suitable."

"I guess," I said.

Shell dug into his wallet and dropped a hundred dollars on the table, more than covering the tab. "You don't seem excited by the prospect. Most of the women I know love to shop."

I put my elbows on the table, resting my face in my hands. "Most of the men I know love to work on cars. I can't imagine you getting grease under your manicure."

He smirked. "Touché. Those who buy Cadillacs can afford to pay someone to tune them up."

"I could have guessed you had a Cadillac."

"I love it. In fact, I love it so much I wouldn't trust a mechanic to tune it up. So I do it myself. And this isn't a manicure." Shell held up his hand, spreading his fingers. "I've been successfully clipping my own nails for years now."

I was surprised, and a little impressed. "I guess we were both wrong to stereotype."

"Agreed. So what is it you do like doing, if I might ask?"

"Competition shooting. I'm the best marksman in the district."

Shell raised an eyebrow. "Marks*man*?"

"The Chicago PD is still getting used to the idea that someone with boobs can shoot. All of my trophies have little gold men in Weaver stances on top of them."

"I bet that pisses off your fellow law enforcement officers."

"It does," I said. "That's why I do it."

Shell stood up, holding out his hand. "So, Officer Streng, are you ready to piss off more of your coworkers by catching this psycho murdering my girls?"

I took Shell's hand. "There's nothing I'd enjoy more."

Present day
2010, August 10

I had to take a break from rubbing the rope against the edge of the concrete. The salt Mr. K had applied had gotten into the raw skin on my wrists, and the pain was otherworldly. I could have worked through the pain, but it was so bad it caused me to cry, and the crying was accompanied by a runny nose.

With the ball gag in my mouth, the only way I could breathe was through my nostrils. A stuffy nose could kill me.

So I rested, keeping still, trying to calm down enough so I could regain control over my emotions. I'd never felt so alone before. The only company I had was the unknown machine humming in the background, and my thoughts and memories.

It would have been okay if there were some good memories mixed with the bad.

Unfortunately, my head was filled with bad stuff that refused to fade away.

Most of the bad stuff revolved around my career. I'd chased, and caught, my share of human monsters. But catching them, or even killing them, didn't bring their victims back. It also didn't make me sleep any better at night.

Before my recent retirement, I'd almost called it quits several times. I never did, but I had come pretty close. In my never-ending quest to prove myself to my coworkers, I'd endured a lot of sexist and chauvinist attitudes. A lot of male cops didn't think women had what it took to work Homicide. It was too ugly for their delicate sensibilities.

In my opinion, it was too ugly for anyone's sensibilities, female or not, delicate or not. But the fact was, women did have a definite disadvantage when working violent crime cases. It didn't have to do with physical brawn or stronger stomachs. It had to do with empathy.

Women in general had the ability to feel the emotions of others. Pain in particular.

I'd seen a lot of pain in my years on the force. It was tough to handle.

Coming upon some horrific crime scene, seeing what some psycho had done to a fellow human being, was difficult for me to cope with. Because I could put myself in their place.

I could see their last moments. The struggling. The fighting. The final breath. I could hear their pleas for mercy. I could feel their fear, their agony, sense their helplessness, imagine their horror so deeply it had led to a lifetime of nightmares. That is, when I could get to sleep at all.

Thinking back over the victims I'd encountered, two stood out as the absolute worst ways a person could die. Both were at the merciless hands of Mr. K.

One was known as the Guinea Worm.

The other, the Catherine Wheel.

Lying there in the storage locker, eyes closed, I couldn't help but shudder at the horrible images they induced.

I also couldn't help but wonder what was making that ominous humming noise next to me.

Three years ago
2007, August 8

When backup arrived at Merle's U-Store-It, there was more vomiting, every time someone new showed up. I got wise and pulled a garbage can over to the scene, but that was about the only wise thing I'd done that day. Even Phil Blasky, who had a stomach made of titanium and could often be seen eating lunch while doing an autopsy, flinched when he saw the body.

"He's been here at least three days," Blasky said during his cursory examination. "Maybe longer. He's wearing an adult diaper. Got two healing IV marks on his arm, where the needle pulled out from the spinning."

According to Blasky, Mr. K had visited the vic at least three times, to change his IV bag, keeping him hydrated and alive during the terrible agony he'd endured.

"Tripod probably held a camcorder," Herb said. "Or maybe a camera taking time-lapse photos. Gives some cred to the theory that Mr. K is a hit man."

I nodded. When the Outfit ordered an execution, they often wanted proof. A picture was a nice memento to keep around to remind you what you did to your enemies. Both Herb and I had worked cases before where videotapes were involved, but those were sex murders. This death didn't appear to have a sexual element. This was about causing as much pain as possible.

The particular torture Mr. K employed dated back to medieval times, where it was known as the Catherine Wheel. It resembled a circus knife-throwing act, where someone was strapped to a large, round board, spread-eagled, and then spun in circles while knives hit the spaces between their limbs. But in this case, there were no thrown knives. The pain came from broken limbs—the victim's arms and legs were each fractured in several places.

For seventy-two hours, a small electric motor had spun him slowly around, his compound fractures stretching and rubbing together, until his arms and legs were so swollen they looked like they'd been inflated.

I couldn't imagine a more horrible way to die.

"Nothing at all. Not a damn thing." Officer Scott Hajek, from the crime scene team, frowned at me. He couldn't find a single shred of evidence anywhere, inside or outside the unit. No fingerprints. No footprints. Even the floor had been swept prior to our arrival. Mr. K didn't leave anything behind.

"Jack, I'd like to talk when you have a sec."

I glanced at Herb, whose fat jowls were hanging down like a basset hound's. Then I nodded and walked him down the hallway.

"I left my post," he said when we were far enough away from the others. "You told me to wait downstairs and watch the exit."

"Herb…"

"I screwed up, Jack. If you want to lodge a formal reprimand—"

"I don't want to lodge a reprimand. Forget about it, Herb."

He stared at me, pained. I tried to keep my face neutral. Because it wasn't Herb's fault. He'd come to my aid when I didn't respond. I was the one who should have exercised some control, told my partner the perp was on his way down.

It wasn't Herb's fault Mr. K got away.

It was mine.

And I deserved more than a reprimand. For letting that monster escape, I felt I deserved to have my badge taken away.

"Let's focus on what to do next," I said, eager to get off the subject of blame. "We've got his car, his plates, his address. We can go talk to him."

"But we didn't catch him in the act, Jack. Did you see him in the locker, with the vic?"

"No," I admitted.

"Did we get a good look at his face when he walked into the building? Can we even put him at the scene?"

This was a common problem with law enforcement. Sometimes, we knew who the bad guy was, but couldn't legally connect him to his crimes. Getting a conviction meant following a specific protocol. If any step along the way wasn't rock solid, the state's attorney wouldn't even attempt to prosecute.

"Dust the elevator," I said. "And the knob on the security door. Let's see if we can get that watchman downstairs to ID him." I had a bad thought. "We should also check to see if our perp has a locker here under his real name."

My worry turned out to be prophetic. The man we followed here did indeed have a storage unit in his name, also on the third floor. Locker 312. That meant he had a reason to be at this facility, and could easily plead innocence in connection with the murder scene. Even if we did find a fingerprint, it wouldn't matter.

Smart guy. Smart, careful, and utterly devoid of humanity.

While Herb called judge after judge, trying to find one who would issue a warrant to search unit 312, I considered our next move.

There was only one. We had to talk to the guy.

It was doubtful he'd give us a full confession. It was doubtful he'd even let us into his home. And if he did let us in, I wasn't sure that was a place I wanted to be.

I'd encountered quite a few psychos in my day. But never one that scared the shit out of me like Mr. K did.

Present day
2010, August 10

"*Hey, Phin. It's Harry.*"

Phineas Troutt rubbed his bleary eyes, wishing he'd checked the caller ID before picking up. He didn't really like Harry McGlade. No one really liked Harry McGlade. But the private detective was bearable in small doses, and they had enough of a history that Phin had a grudging respect for the guy.

Plus, Harry was Jack's new partner, and Jack had told Phin to be nice. While Phin couldn't see how Jack could have gone into the private sector with someone so fundamentally flawed—especially since Jack hated being Harry's partner when they'd been rookies on the force twenty years ago—he respected her wishes. Phin was still adjusting to suburban life, being Jack's live-in boyfriend. It was her house, and she paid all the bills, including paying for his latest round of chemotherapy. If she found some warped sort of satisfaction being McGlade's partner again, Phin wouldn't try to talk her out of it. Even though it personally would have driven him nuts.

"What's up, Harry?"

"Is Jack there?"

"No. She was gone when I woke up this afternoon." Phin still felt a bit nauseous from his treatment yesterday, along with having a whopper of a headache, and was thinking about climbing back into bed as soon as he got off the phone.

"She was supposed to stop by the office so we could divvy up the latest cases. Got one where this guy wants to find out if his mother is cheating on his father with his brother. You can't make shit like that up. Ugly as hell, too. Mom looks like a fat, pink gorilla, but with bigger feet. The son has a face like a carp. I swear, I want to throw a hook in it every time he starts talking. I think people below a certain minimum standard of beauty should have to get a license before they reproduce. A minimum standard of intelligence, too."

He was one to talk on both counts. "I'll tell Jack you called when she gets in touch."

Phin raised his thumb to hit the disconnect button, but Harry's voice continued to drone on.

"I called her four times. Her phone isn't on. Goes right to voice mail."

"Maybe it isn't charged." *Or maybe she just doesn't want to talk to you.*

"You sure she's not there?"

"I'm sure, Harry. I'm alone in the house."

"Did you guys buy a second car?"

"No."

The only car they had was Jack's, a new SUV to replace the Chevy Nova she'd owned for almost half her life. Phin hadn't owned a legitimate car in a while. Before moving in with Jack, the only vehicles he drove were illegally obtained. After being diagnosed with cancer, Phin's concept of morality had become a bit...*skewed* for a time. The only people who knew he lived with Jack were Harry, Jack's mom, and Jack's old partner, Herb Benedict. There were several warrants out for Phin's arrest.

Funny he should wind up falling for a cop.

"Well, you know I put a tracker in Jack's car," Harry said. *"Doesn't hurt to play it safe, especially with her history. According to my GPS, it's still parked in your garage."*

Phin felt a jolt of concern course through him. That same sensation he had while on the street, right before trouble started. He walked through the living room, opened the garage door, and stared at the SUV. In three more steps his hand was on the hood. The engine was cold. But that wasn't what made Phin's heart rate double. The back security door, the one leading to the yard, was missing a section of glass. A neat circle had been cut through it, carefully avoiding the foiled edges that would have set off the house alarm.

"The car is here," Phin said. "When was the last time you talked to Jack?"

"Yesterday."

"Call Herb."

"Herb? I hate that guy. He's like a big, mean walrus."

"Someone broke into the house. I think someone took our girl, Harry. You and Herb meet me here soon as you can. Bring everything you and Jack have been working on lately, and every case going back six months. And tell Herb to bring a list of everyone Jack arrested who just got out of prison."

"I'm on it."

Phin hung up, examining the hole in the window. Jack's home had been invaded before, and she had since beefed up her security. That included foiling the windows—running a paper-thin strip of metal along the perimeter that was hooked up to electricity. If the window was shattered, the alarm went off. The doors also had magnetic sensors, which were supposed to go off if they were opened without a key. A quick look on the outside doorjamb revealed why it hadn't worked; a larger ceramic magnet was stuck to the frame, preventing the mechanism from springing.

Fighting nausea, Phin hurried back into the house. He grabbed the .45 ACP he kept on top of the fridge, jacked a round into the chamber, and shoved it down the back of his jeans. Then he marched down the hallway to the bedroom. The sheets were still tousled from their night of sleep. Phin remembered popping some Compazine for nausea and codeine for pain, half asleep and groggy when Jack finally came to bed—late as she always did, watching infomercials until three a.m.

"How are you feeling, hon?" she'd asked.

"Better, now."

He fell asleep holding her hand.

Staring at the bed now, he tried to imagine someone coming in the room and grabbing Jack while he slept off the effects of the drugs. Why hadn't she struggled? Screamed? The antiemetic and painkillers he took were strong, but if she'd woken him coming to bed, why hadn't she roused him while being dragged off?

Phin rubbed his eyes, then extended the motion down his face and chin, trying to imagine how he would abduct a woman with her lover sleeping beside her. Especially a woman who was a former cop and no doubt had guns in the house.

He examined the bed, the blankets, the pillows, then scanned the carpeting, following it out into the hallway.

There. A smudge of dirt. Faint, no more than two inches long. It repeated, a foot later, and a foot after that, the dash-dash-dash pattern continuing into the kitchen. Phin went back into the hallway and saw the smudge had gotten longer, now a continuous, muddy line. He walked out the back door and into the yard, spying the narrow wheel track in the patch of dirt where the grass had been thin. It hadn't rained last night, but dew collected on the lawn prior to dawn, making it damp.

Phin walked into the tree line, where the grass ended, into a copse of trees. Plenty of places to hide and watch and wait for Jack and her boyfriend to fall asleep.

He folded his arms across his chest, feeling a chill even though it was warm. Then he went back inside and got on Jack's computer. First he checked her e-mail, including her deleted files and spam folder. Without finding anything out of the ordinary, he logged onto Jack's cell phone account and printed out a list of all her recent calls, going back a week. Most of the numbers he recognized, but a few he didn't. Using an online reverse directory, Phin worked his way through several restaurants, cable TV shopping channels, and two unknown numbers that either Herb or Harry could help with.

Then he opened up Firefox and looked at Jack's browsing history. Netflix. Amazon. Clothing retailers. A planned parenthood site.

Phin accessed that and quickly read the page. It was about pregnancy in women over forty.

He left the computer and went to the bathroom, opening the medicine cabinet. He found Jack's birth control pills, ten still left in the pack. Then he checked the garbage can next to the toilet.

An empty box that read "EPT," along with a wrapper for one of the tests.

Phin dug deeper, but the pregnancy test wasn't in there. He went into the kitchen and checked the garbage can under the sink. Nothing.

Where was it? And where was Jack?

Twenty-one years ago
1989, August 16

"So Armani makes clothes for women, too?" I asked Shell, holding the black pantsuit in front of me and staring into the body-length mirror adjacent to Lord & Taylor's fitting rooms.

"It's called a power suit," Shell said. He stood behind me, close enough for me to feel his breath on the back of my head.

"The shoulder pads are too big. I look like I could play defensive tackle for the Bears."

"Try it on. You'll see."

Skeptical, I took the suit, along with a white silk blouse by someone named Ralph Lauren, and slipped into the closest room. Two minutes later, the Sears suit was in piles on the floor around me, and I stepped back out into the store in bare feet and stood in front of Shell and the mirror.

It was like looking at a stranger.

The pants tapered high at the waist and flared out, clinging to my curves, making it obvious this was designed for women. The blouse hugged my breasts, and the shoulder pads

I'd been dubious about made them look bigger than they ever had before.

I was astonished. I actually looked feminine, while still coming across as professional.

More than that, I was hot. Not hot in a slutty way. Hot in a confident, mature, *here's a woman in complete control* way. No wonder it was called a *power suit*.

"Try these on as well."

Shell knelt down next to me, holding a pair of black heels. "These are Givenchy. You're a size seven and a half?"

I nodded, wondering how he knew. Shell gently lifted up my left foot, fit on the strappy heel, and then repeated the process with its twin. Somehow, they made the lines of the suit even stronger.

"What do you think?" he asked, staring up at me.

I turned, looking at it from behind. It was as if Armani had made this especially for me. I'd never felt better wearing any outfit.

"It's amazing," I said.

Shell stood, putting his hand on my neck, finding my ponytail holder. He freed my long, brown hair, and I shook it loose and watched it cascade over my shoulders. I'd gone from being a professional businesswoman, to ready for a night on the town.

"You're beautiful," Shell said.

I'd never been called beautiful before by anyone other than my mother. I was a size six, thanks to the Jane Fonda workout tapes I'd stuck with for the past few years, and my face was okay, but no one would ever put me on the cover of a magazine. Yet when Shell said it, for a brief, magical moment, I believed him. The word made me feel young and girlish and a little bit heady.

"How much is this little ensemble?" I asked. I hadn't checked the tags because I was afraid.

"It doesn't matter. I'm paying."

I turned, facing him. "I make a decent living, Shell. I can buy my own clothes."

"I must insist," he said.

"How much is it?"

"With the shoes, just over nine hundred dollars."

I wasn't sure what to say. That was more than two months' rent.

"That's…a lot of money."

"I learned something a while ago. People don't remember the things you say or do. But they do remember how you look. The better you look, the better impression you make. For a woman in a career dominated by men, you need to make the best impression you can."

I agreed with him completely. But nine hundred bucks? My entire wardrobe didn't cost that much.

"If you prefer, you can pay me back."

The way he said it was a bit oily and suggestive. Almost as if I could pay him back by sleeping with him.

Staring at myself in the mirror, I was seriously considering it.

"I'll let you buy this for me on one condition," I said.

"Name it."

"When we catch the killer, I'm returning it."

"As you wish, Officer. Now we only have one thing left to do."

"And that is?"

Shell grinned. "We have to take some pictures."

75

Three years ago
2007, August 8

John Dalton lived in a condo on 1300 North Lake Shore Drive, in an area known as the Gold Coast, one of the most exclusive—and expensive—parts of the city. He was sixty-two years old and drove a 2006 black Cadillac DTS. He was once in the military, did a tour in Vietnam during the war, had a firearm owner's ID, and a Platinum American Express card, where he listed his occupation as "independent contractor." No criminal record. Not even a parking ticket, which in Chicago was almost unheard of.

Herb and I had been following him earlier that day on a long shot. A week ago, a body had been found in an empty lot on Chicago's South Side, near Seventy-fifth and Evans. The ball gag and salted wounds, coupled with the bizarre method of death, lead to the inevitable Mr. K rumors, and a black DTS was spotted leaving the scene. The murder wasn't in our jurisdiction, but we had nothing else going on and decided to lend a hand.

There were over four hundred vehicles registered in Cook County that matched this description, most of them belonging to limo drivers and car services. Discounting those, women, minorities, and men under a certain age—it had long been assumed Mr. K was a single white male who would now be in his fifties or sixties—that left us with eighteen possibles. We chose to follow Dalton simply based on his driver's license photo. He looked unassuming, but wore a black suit and a black tie that practically screamed *I'm a hit man for the mafia.* Not a very scientific approach to crime-solving on my part, but I'd seen cases broken on smaller hunches.

Now we were faced with the very real possibility that John Dalton really was Mr. K. We didn't have enough evidence for an arrest warrant, or to search his premises, and we were still waiting to hear from the judge if we could get a warrant for the storage locker Dalton had rented.

In the meantime, there was nothing illegal about talking to the guy. At the very least, we needed to ask him if he saw anything at the U-Store-It.

I parked the Nova in front of a fire hydrant on Goethe Street as Herb licked the last bit of cucumber sauce off his fingers. He'd polished off two gyros since we'd left the storage facility, demanding to stop for food since he'd thrown up the bran on the scene.

Me? I never wanted to eat again.

We extracted ourselves from my car—I with more grace than Herb—and I grabbed my laptop. Then we walked toward Lake Shore Drive, to the circular driveway of the condo complex. The outside of the high-rise building was white, balconies facing Lake Michigan, the cheapest of which was worth more than I earned in ten years. The doorman, almost as paunchy as Herb and looking damn uncomfortable in his dark wool uniform, let us in when we showed him our badges. The lobby was plush—carpeting, a sofa, a bank of mailboxes that also boasted a FedEx drop box. Apparently, when the uber-rich wanted something delivered overnight, they didn't want to have to walk very far to send it.

The elevator was fast, and a minute later we were on the twentieth floor knocking on the oak door to unit 20a.

The man who answered was unremarkable. Average height, looks, build. He wore the same black suit we saw him in at the storage facility, but up close I could see it was tailored. His tie was still on, cinched tight on his neck. The bulge in his coat from earlier, the one I thought was a gun, was no longer there. He was clean shaven, the barest hint of gray stubble on his chin. I also noticed his skin was tight—too tight to be natural on a man his age. Mr. Dalton was no stranger to plastic surgery.

He looked at us as a fish might peer out from an aquarium, without interest or expression.

"May I help you, Detectives?"

Herb and I exchanged a glance. Neither of us had told the doorman who we were here to visit, so no doubt Dalton had an arrangement with him, asking to be informed whenever a cop came into the building.

"John Dalton?" I asked.

He didn't answer, nod, or react in the slightest.

"Lieutenant Daniels, Chicago PD. This is my partner, Detective Benedict. We'd like to ask you some questions about your whereabouts earlier today."

"Daniels, you said?" For the first time, his face showed an expression—a slight crinkling around the eyes that might have been amusement. "The Homicide lieutenant?"

My fictionalized exploits had been televised as a grade D television series. I hadn't been portrayed on the show in a positive light.

"May we come in?"

Dalton stepped aside, holding the door for us, then softly closing it. He led us down a short hallway, lined with framed black and white photos. A cornfield. A city skyline. A house on some tropical beach.

The condo was tastefully furnished, cherry wood paneling and floors, Persian rugs, stylish furniture that looked straight from the showroom. Dalton led us into the living room and offered us a sofa facing a bay window with a spectacular lake view. We declined the seat. Then we waited. Waiting is a standard interrogation technique. People find silence uncomfortable and tend to fill it when they can.

Dalton, however, said nothing. He simply stood there, watching us with his slack expression.

"Did you visit Merle's U-Store-It earlier today?" I asked.

"Yes."

"Might I ask why you were there?"

"To store something." Again, a tiny, bemused squint.

"And what did you store?"

"Don't you mean to ask if I stored a dead body there?"

"Why would you say that?" Herb asked, his voice the essence of cool.

"You're Homicide detectives. Am I wrong to assume you're investigating a murder?"

I went with it, curious to see where this would lead. "Did you store a dead body there?"

"Did you see me store a dead body there?"

Herb and I exchanged a look. *Did Dalton know we'd followed him?*

"Please answer the question, Mr. Dalton," I said.

"Now, that would be quite an accomplishment, wouldn't it? Hiding a body in a storage locker. One would probably need a container of some sort. Something on wheels. Or perhaps not. The manager there isn't very attentive, is he? Perhaps a savvy murderer could carry a body in without even being noticed."

"Mr. Dalton, please answer—"

"I'm tired of this question," Dalton said. "Ask me a better one."

I knew Herb felt the same thing I felt. This was our killer. This might even be Mr. K. But we were guests, without a warrant, and although we could probably drag him down to the station to answer questions, no doubt he would lawyer-up and probably sue us and the city. Dalton apparently had money, and he radiated confidence. He wouldn't confess.

But he might screw up if we kept him talking.

"I'd like to show you some pictures on my laptop, Mr. Dalton. It will take a moment."

"Feel free."

I placed the computer on a coffee table and booted up Windows. Then I took a memory stick out of my purse—one that contained the photos from the storage locker crime scene, and the crime scene from Seventy-fifth Street—and accessed my slide show viewer.

The first was of the man found earlier, at the U-Store-It. He hadn't been ID'ed yet. I winced, seeing his misshapen body again.

"Do you recognize him?" Herb asked, taking over because he must have sensed my revulsion.

"I don't. Perhaps I might, if he wasn't so puffy."

"He had his arms and legs broken and was tied to a wheel that spun him around."

"The Catherine Wheel," Dalton said.

"You're familiar with it?" I asked, trying to sound casual.

"I confess a fascination with the macabre, and have quite an extensive collection of books about torture and death, and those who commit such atrocities. I also have several that feature you, Lieutenant. I'm sure there are many who have followed your career. A very many, including some very bad people. May I ask you a question about the Kork family? Is Alex still in prison?"

The Korks were one of the many cases I'd had that still gave me nightmares. That is, when I was even able to get to sleep. "No. A maximum security mental health facility."

"Well, let's hope all of those despicable people you put away never get out. I bet they'd be most upset with you."

"How about this man?" I asked, flipping forward a few jpegs. An ugly image splashed across my desktop, of a crime scene lit with kliegs, illuminating a poor bastard whose intestines had been removed from his body an inch at a time by being wound around a stick.

"Ah, the Guinea Worm," Dalton said. "Quite a terrible way to die."

"You're familiar with it?" Herb asked.

"You know the term *drawn and quartered*? The *drawn* part is being disemboweled. Here, let me show you."

Dalton led me and Herb to a bookcase. He removed a hardcover from the shelf with the title *The History of Torture and Punishment,* and quickly flipped to a page that showed a graphic drawing of a man in agony, his insides being pulled out. The caption below read "Guinea Worm."

"There is a parasite known as the guinea worm," Dalton said, "which gets into the bloodstream and then bursts out of a vein in the leg. The only way to remove the creature is to tie it to a stick and slowly pull it out, bit by bit. Imagine someone doing the same thing with your intestines. Most painful."

I was stunned. This man was practically telling us he did it. Was he presenting some sort of warped challenge to us? Daring the police to catch him?

Next he turned to a full-page sketch of someone dying on the Catherine Wheel.

"I bet the two could be combined," Dalton said. "As the victim turned, his intestines could also be wound around a stick. The best of both worlds."

I looked away, eyeing some of his other books. They were all true crime, except for two novels. One was called *Blue Murder*. The other, *The Passenger*.

Dalton noticed my gaze. "Are you familiar with author Andrew Z. Thomas?"

I nodded. "A bestselling thriller writer. He became a serial killer."

"He allegedly joined forces with another killer named Luther Kite. They were both involved in the Kinnakeet Ferry Massacre of 2003, among other unsavory murders."

I remembered the crime back when it came over the wires, and I still recalled the pictures of the duo. Thomas was average-looking, not the serial killer type at all. But Luther looked like he stepped out of a horror movie. Gaunt, pale face. Dark eyes. Black, greasy hair.

"How about this one?" Herb asked, pulling a title from the shelf.

The book was a dog-eared paperback entitled *Unknown Subject K*.

"Yes, I've heard of him. Supposedly, he's killed more than the top ten other famous murderers put together. Some think he's an urban legend, created by the FBI." Dalton stared at me, his eyes crinkling. "What do you think, Lieutenant?"

"I think he's make-believe," I said carefully. "No one could have committed all of the atrocities that have been attributed to him."

Now Dalton actually did grin. It was small, no more than a slight upturn of his lips, and seemed oddly out of place on his emotionless face. "Are you sure about that?"

"Did you recognize the man in the last photo I showed you, Mr. Dalton?" I asked, despising his smile.

"The Guinea Worm fellow?"

"The man has been identified as Jimmy 'The Nose' Gambucci. He was a member of the Lambini crime family. Do you have any associations with organized crime?"

"Are you asking if I could call up Tony Lambini, have him talk to his powerful friends, and get you fired? Why would I do that, Lieutenant? Do you perceive yourself as a threat to me?"

This conversation had gone from bizarre to downright surreal.

"Mr. Dalton," I said, figuring I had nothing to lose. "Are you Mr. K?"

Dalton touched his index finger to his chin, then pointed it at his hallway. "Did you see my photographs, when you were coming in? The one on the end is of my chateau in Cape Verde. It's one of the few hospitable countries in the world that doesn't have extradition treaties with the United States. Do you know what that means?"

"It means bad guys can go there," Herb said, "and we're not allowed to bring them back."

"A gold star for the chubby sidekick," Dalton said. Then he turned to me. "I've worked hard for my entire life, Ms. Daniels, and am ready for retirement. I'm leaving for Cape Verde tomorrow. After I go, I don't plan on ever returning.

If I am this elusive Mr. K, you have a little over twenty-four hours to come up with enough evidence to arrest me, or else I'm afraid his identity will forever remain a mystery to all but a select few."

I replayed everything he'd said since we'd walked in. Was it enough to take him down to the station? If so, would it be enough to get a warrant to search his house?

No. Dalton hadn't actually admitted to anything. And I had no doubt he'd be free an hour after I brought him in.

"Let me tell you what I think of Mr. K," I said evenly. "He's a parasite, just like a guinea worm. And like the guinea worm, he needs to be drawn out into the open and exterminated."

Dalton leaned in close. "I've followed your lackluster career, Lieutenant. You aren't good enough to catch him."

"We'll see."

I picked up my laptop and left the condo with Herb at my heels, swearing to myself I'd put this creep away if it was the last thing I ever did.

Present day
2010, August 10

Controlling my breathing was the first step. Once I slowed that down, I was able to stop crying, relax my cramping muscles, and think through the panic.

My wrists were ridiculously sore, as if someone had branded them with hot irons. I wiggled my fingers, keeping the circulation going, and then tried to reason out my situation.

Mr. K had me. That was obvious. But I didn't see how that could be possible. Too much didn't make sense.

Could it be a copycat? Someone imitating Mr. K?

I wished I could remember how I got into the storage locker. My last memory was watching infomercials in the living room, Phin asleep in bed. He was doing another round of chemo after an ultrasound had found another tumor on his pancreas. How long ago was that? A few hours? A day?

I must have been drugged. That would explain the loss of memory.

Could Mr. K somehow have tracked me down and—

The loud *CLICK!* was accompanied by an explosion of light. I slammed my eyelids closed, but the glare still burned my corneas, causing an instant headache. After a few seconds, I peeked through the painful brightness, squinting at the spotlight hanging on the wall.

Blinking away motes and halos, I began to look around. I was in a storage locker, as I'd guessed. Metal walls. A metal door. The concrete block I was tethered to was larger than I'd assumed, at few hundred pounds at least. I swiveled my head around, looking for the machine making the whirring noise.

When I saw it, my whole body clenched.

It was a wheel. A large, spinning wheel, with straps for a person's arms and legs.

The Catherine Wheel.

But this one was unlike any I'd seen before. Attached to it was a metal pole, which looked like the rotating spit from a gas grill.

I immediately knew what it was. I remembered John Dalton's description of the Guinea Worm, and I could picture someone strapped to the wheel, their broken bones grinding together, while the turning metal bar slowly disemboweled them.

Next to the wheel, on the floor, was a digital clock. It was counting down the seconds.

1:59:43…1:59:42…1:59:41…

After a brief, internal battle to squelch panic, panic won out. I screamed into the gag. Screamed until my throat was raw, until the tears came again, until I was hyperventilating so badly that I passed out.

Twenty-one years ago
1989, August 16

I didn't take Shell up on his offer to shoot some pictures of me back at his place. He was cute, smart, and almost predatory with his sexuality. While I liked the confident, lothario vibe he gave off, and the attraction was no doubt mutual, I wasn't going to screw up my first real case by, well, screwing one of the people involved.

So I took him to my place instead.

He had one of those expensive SLR cameras with an assortment of lenses and filters, portable lights, and even a stand-up backdrop, all in the trunk of his Caddy. While he was setting up in my living room, I went into my bathroom and futzed around with makeup. While I wasn't Max Factor, I managed to slap enough color on my face to look feminine. Then I ran a brush through my hair and hit it with Aquanet, trying to tease it up as big as possible. By the time I was finished, I looked like I could be in a Whitesnake video.

Then I changed out of my Sears suit and put on the outfit Shell had bought for me. All dolled up, it was hard for me to recognize the person in the mirror. It didn't look much like me. Rather, it looked more like the person I wanted to be.

I finished off the can of Aquanet, choking on the aerosol, and then walked out of the bathroom. My apartment was small, even by civil servant standards, so the bathroom let out right into the living room, where Shell had erected a makeshift studio, complete with three-point lighting. A white screen, with back splashes of red and blue lights, was set up in front of my television.

"Wow," he said as I approached.

I thought of my boyfriend, Alan. He never said *wow* when he saw me.

"Would you like a drink?" I asked. I wasn't sure why, but I suddenly felt a tiny bit uncomfortable.

"Whiskey, if you've got it."

"Hate the stuff," I said. "Vodka okay?"

"Rocks."

I went into the kitchen, opening the cabinet and hoping I had two matching rocks glasses. I didn't. The only matching glasses I owned had Ronald McDonald on them. I gave Shell my single rocks glass, then poured my vodka up, in a martini glass, making sure he wasn't looking at the bargain basement brand I was serving. I dropped two ice cubes in his and then went into the living room. After handing him his drink, I realized why I was nervous. Having a cute guy in my apartment felt like a date. We'd gotten very comfortable with each other very quickly. Too quickly.

I took a very small sip of vodka, set it on a bookcase, and put my hands on my hips.

"Okay," I said. "Let's do this."

Shell finished his drink in one gulp, and if he noticed it was sub-par vodka he didn't show it. "Stand in front of the backdrop," he told me.

Immediately, I felt like I was back in high school, getting a class photo. I always hated those, standing in front of some disinterested, impatient photographer who didn't want to be there, nervous that I'd look goofy.

"Have you been shot before?" Shell asked.

"Shot at, but they missed," I said, before realizing what he was asking. A moment later we both laughed, and the camera went *click, click, click.*

"The secret to getting terrific shots is to pretend the camera is a person you like. You want to show this person how much you like him, how interested you are in him. How you want him to see you. So right now, tell the camera *hello* with your eyes."

It sounded like utter bullshit, but I gave it a try. Shell snapped a few pics, then told me to pout, like the camera broke a date with me. I tried it, jutting out my lower lip a bit, trying to channel my inner spoiled brat.

From pouty we went to flirty, then to serious, then to curious. Soon we were in a comfortable rhythm and I no longer flinched at the shutter sounds. Shortly after that, I no longer paid any attention to Shell. The world had been reduced to me and the camera. The camera told me what it wanted, and I tried to please the camera.

"Let's take off the jacket...

"Show me coy...

"Let's untuck one shirttail...

"Show me thoughtful...

"Let's open the blouse a button or two...

"Show me daring...

"Let's open it one more button...

"Show me turned on."

At that last suggestion, I lost all momentum. "Excuse me?" I asked.

"Turned on," Shell said. "Aroused. You know. Your sex face."

The inner vamp I was channeling was now confused and embarrassed. "My portfolio will have a picture of my sex face?"

Shell released the camera, letting it hang by its strap. "I'm not talking mouth-open eyes-shut *When Harry Met Sally*. I mean that look you give your boyfriend when you're really aroused. Your *take me now* look."

I didn't think I had a *take me now* look.

"Don't you have enough shots?" I asked. "You went through three rolls."

"I've got some good ones. Some great ones. But I don't have the *knock a man on his ass* shot yet. Do you trust me?"

"I don't know." I tried for a laugh, but it came out more like a nervous squeak.

"Just keep your eyes on the camera and listen to my words." Shell raised it to his face. "We've just had a terrific dinner and are eating dessert. Strawberries and fresh cream. I dip a strawberry in the cream and feed it to you. But I don't give it to you right away. I just dab the berry on your bottom lip, teasing you. I run it along your teeth, gently, before pushing the tip of it inside. Then you feel my hand caress your thigh under the table."

Rather than sounding creepy, Shell's voice was oddly hypnotic. I could see the scene. Feel the cold cream in my mouth. The tart sweetness of the fruit. A warm hand on my leg.

"You reach out to bite the strawberry, but I pull it away."

My lips parted, just a bit.

"Imagine you want the berry in your mouth. How would you tell me that with your eyes?"

I felt my eyes smolder a bit. He snapped some pictures.

"Now my fingers are moving slowly up your thigh. I touch the edge of your panties. I keep them there, rubbing them back and forth, back and forth, waiting for your signal to put them inside. Show me you want me to."

It was easier than I thought it would be, because I was getting turned on. I tried to remember the last time I'd had sex. It had been a few weeks. Alan and I were having a dry spell, worsened by him traveling a lot and my long hours. I'd also been too busy to take care of myself lately, and having a man—an attractive man with a camera—talk in deep, dulcet tones about rubbing my thigh was more than enough to get me going.

"That's it," Shell said. "That's the look." He set down the camera and stared at me.

"But I haven't knocked you on your ass," I breathed.

I walked up to him, taking my time, liking the way his eyes were on my body. Then I touched his camera lens, running my finger along it, feeling deliciously wicked.

Shell grabbed me abruptly, cupping my ass in his hand, pulling me close, so close I could feel he was just as turned on as I was.

I realized it was wrong, but I tilted up my head to be kissed anyway. He lowered his lips to mine but stopped short, only a few millimeters away. Shell gently kissed one side of my mouth, and the other. Then he softly chewed on my lower lip, tasting like vodka and heat.

Shell's tongue sought mine, met it, and I moaned in my throat.

That's when my front door opened and my boyfriend, Alan, walked in.

Present day
2010, August 10

Phin showed Herb Benedict and Harry McGlade the mud lines on the carpeting in the hallway.

"He must have wheeled in a gas canister on a hand truck," Phin said. "Stuck the tube under the door and filled the bedroom. That's why he didn't wake us up when he took Jack."

"So he's a doctor?" Herb asked. He was jotting things down in his notebook. "He has access to anesthetics?"

"Not necessarily," Phin said. "You can get nitrous oxide—laughing gas—at any welding supply store. When I woke up, I had a metallic taste in my mouth that could have been nitrous."

Herb blinked at McGlade, who was staring at him. "What?"

"Every time I see you, you have another chin," Harry said.

Herb scowled. "Have you taken your pill today?" he asked.

"What pill?"

"Your *shut the fuck up* pill."

Harry's brow crinkled. "Where did I hear that before?"

"Guys, stay focused," Phin said.

Herb gave McGlade a lingering glare, then turned back to Phin. "How did he know when you went to sleep?"

"He was watching the house. Or maybe a listening device."

"I'll check for bugs," McGlade said. "I brought my spy gear."

He set a metal suitcase on the floor and opened it up, spilling contents all over the carpet. One of the items that rolled away was a sex toy.

"That's spy gear?" Herb said, pointing at the pink dildo.

"It's got a listening device in it. I swapped it with a woman's vibrator and put it in her desk drawer, trying to catch her cheating on her husband."

"Did it work?" Phin asked.

McGlade frowned. "I got the switches mixed up. All I recorded was three hours of *bzzzz-zzzz...oh God...bzzzz...oh my God...bzzzz*. I should have put a camera in it, too."

"You're an idiot," Herb said.

"And you're a miracle of evolution," Harry replied. "Somehow a sea cow grew limbs and learned how to talk."

Phin stepped between them. "Harry, put away the dildo microphone. Herb, unclench your fists. Do either of you have any idea who could have Jack?"

Herb let out a slow breath, then shook his head. "Not so far. We normally get alerts when someone we put away gets out. All the major ones are still in there. Got a few baddies who were up for parole recently, but they were all denied."

"Were there any cases Jack was working on before she quit? Any open cases?"

Herb's brow crinkled. "Only one. But it couldn't be him."

"Harry? Were you and Jack working on anything?"

"Nothing big." McGlade picked up a slim black case with an antenna sticking out of it. "Bug detector," he said. Then he held it next to Herb and said, "Beep, beep, beep! Crab lice alert!"

Herb shoved the device away, then got behind Harry and roughly pressed him up against the wall. "You keep it up, and the next thing your magic dildo is going to record is you going *pbbthhhh* when I shove it up your—"

"Enough," Phin said, pulling Herb off of McGlade. "I will personally kick both your asses if you don't cut this shit out and focus. Harry, have you noticed anything weird lately? Strange phone calls? E-mails?"

"There is the one guy, keeps e-mailing me, telling me I won the Nigerian lottery. I'm thirty percent sure it isn't legit."

Phin forced himself to unclench his own fists. The best way to deal with Harry was excruciating patience. "Seen anyone hanging around the office? Anyone following you or Jack?"

McGlade's eyes lit up. "Actually, there was this one guy. A few days ago. Spooky looking mother. Black, greasy hair. Pale as the sickly, white underbelly of a morbidly obese sea cow."

"Where did you see him?"

"Outside the office. Just standing on the corner, staring up at our window."

"Did Jack see him?" Phin asked.

Harry scrunched his eyes closed. "No. She was on the phone with a client. I was playing FarmVille—I just earned enough from my turnip patch to buy a tractor—and I noticed him down there. Checked again a few minutes later, and he was still there."

"What did you do then?"

"I plowed my field in like one-tenth of the time. That tractor is epic."

Herb began searching the floor, and Phin guessed he was going to make good on his threat.

"Did you go down and talk to him?" Phin asked Harry.

"Naw. When I checked again, he was gone. Hey, how come we aren't Facebook friends?"

"Because I'm not on Facebook," Phin said. "I actually have a life."

"You should get on there, and friend me, and then send me fuel for my new tractor."

Now Phin got in McGlade's personal space, backing him up against the same wall Herb had shoved him against.

McGlade's eyes went wide. "Hey, easy buddy."

"If you kill him," Herb said, "I'll call it suicide in the police report."

"You're not taking this seriously, McGlade." Phin spoke softly. "Someone has Jack. We need to stop screwing around."

"Relax, Phin. How many times have we been in this situation? So many times, we already know how it's going to end. It'll be a close call, but me, or you, or Tubby the Talking Manatee here will save her at the last possible second. That's what always happens."

"Strangle him," Herb said. "We'll make it look like autoerotic asphyxiation."

"Check the house for bugs, Harry," Phin ordered. "And don't say another goddamn word."

Phin released him. Harry smoothed out his rumpled suit and said, "When I win the Nigerian lottery, I'm not giving either of you a penny." Then he turned on his bug detector and walked into the bedroom.

"We might need help on this one," Phin said to Herb.

"Way ahead of you. Every cop on the force who ever met Jack Daniels is on the lookout for her. They're not going to let one of their own slip away."

Phin nodded. He knew how hard Jack worked, all of those years on the street, trying to earn the respect of her peers. Having them rally behind her would have made her feel good.

"The media?" Phin asked.

"We're keeping it on the down low for now. If some psycho does have her, we don't want to egg him on with press. Have you considered this might be someone new?"

"You mean, like a ransom thing?"

"Maybe. Or maybe some unknown whack-job read about her and wanted to get his name in the true crime books."

Phin didn't like that scenario at all. If it was someone from Jack's past, at least they had a chance at finding her. How could they find someone completely new?

"The bedroom is clean," Harry said, returning to the hall. "Except for those sheets. I saw several stains of dubious origin."

"Check the rest of the house," Phin said.

"Kidnaper might have also been watching from outside," Harry said. "In one of those Hannibal Lector movies, the killer watched the house from the backyard and left all sorts of easy-to-follow clues behind."

"Finish in here," Phin said, "and Herb and I will check outside."

Phin led the portly cop through the garage, out the back door. He located the tire track in the mud, then followed the direction of the treads back into the tree line.

"Take the left side," Phin said. "I'll take the right."

Phin waded into the bushes. After four steps, he had to hold up his bare arms so they didn't brush the nettles. Turning around, he saw there was no good view of the house—it was too obscured by foliage. He looked up, scanning the trees, finding one nearby.

At the base of the tree, half-hidden by the nettles, were two empty boxes of candy. Lemonheads. They appeared relatively new. No sun bleaching, and they were dry even though it had rained two days ago.

Phin let his eyes wander up the tree, and found a low-hanging limb. Though he wasn't feeling his best, he managed to get up onto the bough. From there, he could see over the bushes, a direct line of sight to the bedroom window. Jack insisted on always keeping the shades closed, but it would be easy to tell if the lights were on or off.

"Found something!"

Phin looked over at Herb, who was thirty yards away, in the bushes near the garage. As he was getting down he found a Lemonhead candy stuck in the tree bark. He left it there and walked over to Herb.

"Footprints, right here." Herb pointed at the ground. "Also some twigs broken off the bush so it was easier to see the house.

"Back there, someone was in a tree. You thinking two vantage points?"

"Either two vantage points," Herb said, "or two abductors."

They walked the perimeter of the property, trying to see if anyone else could have been watching. All they found were old, spent shell casings—the reason Jack now insisted on keeping the shades drawn, and why she'd installed the new burglar alarm. But there was no evidence of recent surveillance, except in those two spots.

Herb and Phin went back into the house. Harry was in the kitchen. He'd made himself a submarine sandwich and was finishing a bite. "No bugs in the refrigerator," he said, mouth full.

"How about the rest of the house, jackass?" Herb said.

McGlade stared at Herb and protectively hid the sandwich behind his back. "Whole house is clean. At least, it was."

Harry pointed his chin to the floor, which was dotted with nettles Phin had dragged in. Phin pondered that for a moment, wondering if it meant something. Wondering what they were supposed to do next.

Three years ago
2007, August 8

"What are we supposed to do next?" Herb asked.

We were exiting Dalton's building and walking back to my Nova.

"The only thing we can do," I answered. "We watch him. Follow him. Hope he makes a move."

"You think he'll make a move?" We waited for a cab to pass, then crossed the street. "He's leaving the country tomorrow. You think he'll do something to screw that up?"

"I think he's a disturbed old guy who wants to play some kind of game. And if he does screw up, I want to be there."

I unlocked my car, started the engine, and cranked on the air-conditioning. The chassis rocked when Herb sat down. After checking for traffic, I pulled out onto the street, turned onto Lake Shore Drive, and parked next to the 1300 building, near the underground garage. It didn't matter if Dalton saw us—he practically challenged us to follow him, and no doubt knew we would.

I called a detective in my district, Tom Mankowski, and asked him to check the passenger lists on all flights to Cape Verde over the next three days, looking for Dalton's name. I also asked him if he could confirm Dalton had a residence there.

Then we waited.

"So how's Latham doing?" Herb asked. "Fully recovered yet?"

"He's good."

Latham, my fiancé, was still recuperating from a bout with botulism. He was almost back to normal, and we were going on vacation later in the month, renting a cabin on Rice Lake in Wisconsin. I had to testify at a murder trial next week, but that wouldn't take more than a day or two. Then I was free of police work for seven glorious days. Though, knowing my luck, I'd probably run into some psychopath during the trip.

"How's the wife?" I asked Herb.

"Good."

We kept waiting.

"Think we've run out of things to talk about?" Herb asked.

"No, not at all," I answered.

Neither of us spoke for fifteen minutes. We watched a bike courier ride up to Dalton's building. He unhooked a bag attached to his rear bumper with bungee cords, and walked past the doorman.

"Remember when we first met?" Herb asked.

"Not really."

"Sure you do. It was with that guy...the escort murder guy. Shell."

"Can we talk about something else?" I didn't like thinking about Shell.

"Sorry. Didn't know it was still a soft spot."

"It's not," I lied. "What about it?"

"That was eighteen years ago. We've been working together for a long time."

"Sure have."

"I've probably spent more time with you than I have with my wife."

My eyes wandered away from the building and over to Herb. "You're not going to tell me you're in love with me, are you Herb?"

Herb smirked. "I wouldn't want to ruin what you've got going on with Latham."

"That's kind of you, because I'd hate to break up your marriage."

"Also, and I don't mean this to be an insult—"

"Translation: here comes the insult."

"—but you're a little too much like one of the guys. It would be like sleeping with my brother."

"You have a brother? And he has boobs?"

"We're getting off tangent here. What I wanted to say was—"

"I want to hear about your D-cup brother."

"—we've been partners for a long time—"

"Is he my size? Maybe we could swap designer clothes."

"—and you're my best friend."

His words sunk right through my skin, into my bone marrow, where they nestled warmly.

"Really?" I said. "Best friend?"

"Really. I just wanted to say that. And it's okay if you don't say it back."

"Herb, I don't want to burst your bubble, here—"

"Please don't hurt my feelings, Jack. I break easily."

"—but this isn't the first time you've said this to me."

"Yeah, it is."

"Herb, you say this whenever we go out and you have more than five drinks."

He raised an eyebrow. "Seriously?"

"Not the part about your brother with the rack, but the best friend bit."

"Do not."

"Do too. Has to be over a dozen times now." I looked at him. "Have you been hitting the sauce today?"

"Not yet. But I may step out and get a bottle of something to kill my embarrassment."

"Counterproductive. Halfway into the bottle, you'll be pouring your heart out to me again, wanting to get matching T-shirts and friendship bracelets."

We waited some more.

"Jack?" Herb said after a few minutes.

"Yeah?"

"So when I've had too many drinks, and I say this to you..."

"Yeah?"

"How do you respond?"

I looked him straight in the eyes. "That you're my best friend too, and I love you like a sister."

"You have a sister? And she has a penis?"

"We should set her up with your brother," I said. "They'd be perfect for each other."

"They'd probably just wind up being friends. Hey, there's the Caddy."

Herb pointed, and sure enough Dalton's DTS was on the move. He squealed tires, swinging onto the road, fishtailing before rocketing forward.

I threw the car into drive and gunned the engine. Hitting the gas in my Nova was akin to yelling at a mouse on a treadmill in an attempt to make it run faster. There were no squealing tires when I pulled out after him, and the engine made a sound somewhere between a whine of pain and a resigned sigh of defeat. I turned onto Division Street, hoping for a tailwind.

"Remind me again why we take your car," Herb said.

"Just keep your eye on him."

"He's too far ahead. I think he just crossed the border into Pennsylvania."

My Nova moved noticeably faster when Herb wasn't in the car, but I didn't say anything and risk insulting my bestest friend.

"I think he turned," Herb said.

"Where?"

"Up there, at the Washington Monument."

"You're funny, like oral thrush is funny."

We drove another block.

"Try pressing the accelerator," Herb suggested.

"I am pressing the accelerator."

"Do you need me to open the hood, wind the rubber band?"

"It's not a rubber band," I said, passing a minivan. "It's a mouse on a treadmill."

"I think your mouse is sleeping. Or dead."

I tapped the brakes and hit the horn to tell a cabbie what I thought of his driving, but the horn didn't want to respond. "Where'd he turn?"

"Clybourn. Right."

"Do you think he's—?"

"Yeah. I do."

We were heading straight for Merle's U-Store-It. Was Dalton trying to clear out his storage locker? What if he did it before we got there?

"Put the cherry on the roof," I said. A little while back, my antique stick-on police siren had fallen off, and I'd been given a slightly less-antique siren. Instead of a suction cup, this new one had a magnet to keep it attached.

"Where is it?" Herb asked.

"On the floor, behind my seat."

Herb took a glance at his expansive waistline, then at me. "You're kidding, right? I can't reach that."

"Pretend it's a big box of cupcakes."

"What kind of cupcakes?"

The light ahead of me turned red, but I blew through it anyway, narrowly missing a sideswipe by an overeager bus driver.

"Recline your seat," I told him, swerving around the bus. The Cadillac was long out of sight, but I knew where the storage place was. Worst case, we'd get there two, maybe three minutes behind him.

Herb pulled the lever and his seat immediately snapped backward. "I can see the siren," he said. "I think I can reach it."

He made a strange grunting sound, sort of like an elephant trumpeting, as he stretched behind me for the light. I turned into oncoming traffic to pass some idiot driving the speed limit and following the rules of the road.

"Got it." Herb blew out a big breath. "Whew. Got any Gatorade?"

"Now sit up and attach it to my roof," I said, inching the Nova up to forty-five.

"Sit what now?"

"Up, Herb. Haven't you ever watched those shows about those morbidly obese people who haven't gotten out of bed in five years?"

"Those shows make me hungry."

Herb had the siren cradled in his prodigious lap. I had ten white knuckles on the steering wheel and couldn't pull them off to help him.

"Come on, partner," I urged. "Crank down the window—"

"You have manual windows? When was this car made, during the Depression?"

"—and stick the cherry on my roof. You can do it."

There was heaving. Grunting. Swearing. And labored, strangled breathing which—if witnessed by a doctor—would have resulted in the crash cart being wheeled over, stat. But somehow Herb managed to get that window open.

"Good work. Now sit up and stick it on the roof."

"You're driving too fast. I can't get the seat up."

"Come on, Herb. You can do this. Say it. Believe it."

"Okay."

"You can do this."

"I can do this."

"You got it."

"I got it."

"You're the man."

"I. Am. The man."

Herb held the cherry out the window, then immediately dropped it outside. I checked my rearview and watched it bounce off the street, where it splintered into a million little red and blue pieces.

"I owe you a siren," Herb said.

I frowned. "I never even got to try it."

"Don't worry. I'll call Starsky and Hutch and get you a new one."

I turned onto Fullerton, seeing that Dalton's Cadillac was already parked across from the storage place. I hit the brakes right next to the building.

"Put in your earpiece," I told Herb, screwing my Bluetooth into my ear. "Guard the exit unless I call for help."

Herb managed to sit up and he nodded, reaching for his pocket. I exited the car and ran into the storage building. The same watchman was there, feet up on his small desk, eyeballs sewn onto the TV screen. I banged on his bulletproof glass.

"Police. Buzz me in."

"Got a warrant?" he asked, not bothering to look at me.

"Open the goddamn door, pinhead!"

He buzzed me in. I hurried to the elevator, saw it was on the third floor. Once again I trudged up the stairs, tugging out my Colt, feeling a weird sort of déjà vu that wasn't déjà vu at all because I had actually done this before, earlier today.

"Where are you?" Herb, in my ear.

"Coming up on the third floor," I said, taking the stairs two at a time. "Check out his car. See if there's anything in it. Be discreet."

By *discreet* I meant *don't get caught inside without a warrant.*

I stopped at the doorway, crouched, and went through low. First I looked left, and saw John Dalton standing four yards away, hands at his sides, looking at me. His expression was neutral, his stance relaxed. I kept my gun aimed at the floor.

"Hello, Lieutenant," he said. "I've been expecting you."

I straightened up to my full height, then walked slowly to him. "Open your jacket, Mr. Dalton. Slowly."

"I just came to clear out my storage locker before leaving the country," he said, unbuttoning his suit coat and opening it up. Then he turned in a full circle. "I'm unarmed."

"Coat pocket," I said. "A bulge. Reach in and take it out with two fingers."

"As you wish." He stuck his thumb and index finger into his jacket and slowly removed a microcassette recorder. I could see the tiny wheel turning. "I thought we should record our conversation, for posterity."

I glanced quickly at Dalton's right, saw his storage locker, 312, was open. I approached, my weapon still out, my senses all on high alert. As I got nearer, I was able to peer inside his rental unit.

"His car is locked," Herb said. "Don't see anything inside. Also, two men just pulled up in a Mercedes."

"You look a bit high-strung, Lieutenant," Dalton said. "I assure you, there's nothing to fear. At least, not at the moment."

Looking into the storage unit, it appeared empty. No... not empty. There was something small resting in the middle of the bare floor.

"You have my permission to go in and take whatever you want," Dalton said. "It's for you anyway. A parting gift, of a sort."

I took him up on his invitation, walking into the locker. On the floor was a cheap digital watch, the kind with a black plastic band sold in drugstores, and a white envelope. I holstered my gun and dug two latex gloves out of my jacket pocket. Keeping an eye on Dalton, I pulled on the gloves and reached for the watch.

"The men are going into the building, Jack," Herb said. *"Want me to follow?"*

"Run their plates," I said, squinting at the watch display.

Instead of showing the time, the gray LCD was counting down from twenty-four hours and thirty-six minutes.

24:36:19...24:36:18...

"What happens when this reaches zero?" I asked.

"Don't ticking clocks just make everything more dramatic?"

"Answer the question, John."

"Open the envelope, Jack."

Inside was a color photograph. It showed a boy, Caucasian, perhaps twelve years old. A close-up, his whole face filling the shot. He had brown hair, brown eyes, and looked like a million other kids. His lips were curled up in a small, private smile, as if he had a joke he wanted to tell.

"Who is this?" I asked, staring over at Dalton.

"What would you do, Lieutenant, if you knew how much time you had left? If you knew, to the very second? What would your final thoughts be before saying goodbye?"

I felt myself going from jittery to cold. "What are you telling me?"

"I'm saying that we can only be here for so long. For some, it could be years before we leave. For others, it could be just over twenty-four and a half hours."

I turned the photo over. On the back, in black marker, was written:

$$515$$

"What have you done here, John?"

"I'm leaving the country tomorrow. There are over one thousand storage facilities in Chicago, and another thousand in the surrounding suburbs. Good hunting, Jack."

The elevator dinged behind me. Two men in suits got out. I put my hand on my holster.

"Who are these guys, Herb?"

"Still checking their plates," he answered.

I watched the men spot us and begin to walk over. Their suits were tailored, expensive. They didn't seem to be carrying.

"Are you saying, John, that this child only has twenty-four hours left to live?" I asked, watching the new arrivals.

"My client is saying no such thing," one of the men said.

"Car belongs to a lawyer, Jack," Herb buzzed in my ear. *"Name is Simon Bradstreet."*

I knew of Simon Bradstreet. He defended all the big mobsters in Chicago.

"I invited Mr. Bradstreet here to make sure my rights and personal freedoms weren't violated," Dalton said. "The Chicago Police Department has a nasty reputation for coercion. I know you aren't the type to beat a confession out of a suspect, Lieutenant, but one never knows how do-gooders will react when children are involved."

"Want me to come up, Jack?" Herb said.

I thought it through. Dalton hadn't actually said he'd abducted a child, or that the child was in danger. He'd carefully chosen his words, and he'd recorded our entire exchange. I had no evidence to arrest him, and I couldn't question him without his consent.

But at the same time, I couldn't let this bastard leave if he had a child locked in a storage facility somewhere. What I needed was to stall.

"It's great of you coming out to this part of town at the request of a client," I said. "But this isn't the best neighborhood. Both of you are driving such nice cars. I'd hate to see them vandalized. Tires slashed. That sort of thing."

"Are you threatening to slash our tires?" Bradstreet said. He barked a fake laugh, his chubby face jiggling.

"I'm doing no such thing," I said, speaking slowly. "And how could I, since I'm here talking to you? All I'm saying is it would be unfortunate if it happened."

"Are we done here?" Bradstreet said.

"I have a question for your client, before you go."

"Mr. Dalton isn't answering any questions."

"I think he'll want to answer this one." I turned to Dalton. "Do you believe in evil, John?"

"I said, Mr. Dalton is not—"

Dalton held up his hand, shushing his lawyer. "Evil, Jack? In what sense do you mean?"

"I had this question posed to me years ago, when I was a cadet. Which is true evil? Someone who enjoys committing evil acts? Or someone who commits evil acts for monetary gain?"

Dalton made a steeple out of his fingers. "Let me tell you a story. About two men. They both worked for…let's call it a company. One of these men enjoyed committing evil acts. He enjoyed it a great deal. So much so that the only way to ever stop him from doing it was to put him away forever, or kill him. The other man, he learned early in life that killing was something he was good at. But he never had any passion for it. In fact, he never had much passion for anything. This lack of emotion, however, made him very good at what he did. Smart. Careful. Deliberate. Because he knew that once emotion got involved, mistakes could be made."

"What happened to these two men?" I asked.

"You know what happened to the first one. As for the second one, we won't truly know what happens for at least twenty-four more hours."

He turned to leave. "But which one is more evil, John?"

Dalton glanced at me over his shoulder. "There's no good or evil, Jack. Each of us is the hero in the movie of our life. The only difference is that some of us are better at justifying our actions to ourselves, while others beat themselves up for every mistake they make."

The trio walked away. And there wasn't a damn thing I could do about it.

Present day
2010, August 10

He stares at the iPhone screen. It's much easier to see Jack Daniels now that the lights are on. That green night vision was blurry and didn't allow for much detail.

But now, the details are perfect. Crystal clear. He even has controls to zoom in. To pan. To tilt. It's amazing how far technology has come, and it's thrilling for him to see this woman, his nemesis, bound and gagged and waiting for the pain to begin.

She's sleeping. Or pretending to.

Rest now, he thinks. *Enjoy unconsciousness while you can, whore.*

Then he slips his hand inside his underwear and watches, a line of drool dripping down his chin, waiting for Jack to wake up.

Twenty-one years ago
1989, August 16

"Jack?"

"Alan!" I quickly pulled away from Shell, wondering if my boyfriend had seen us kissing. "Hi!"

Alan's face screwed up in confusion. He wore the standard Alan outfit: acid-washed jeans, a blue iZod shirt, the pennies in his loafers nice and coppery bright. His thick, wavy blond hair was long in the back, the bangs short and hugging his tan forehead. In his hand he had a dozen roses, which made me feel positively awful.

"Did I…come at…a bad time?" Alan said, sizing up Shell.

"Is this your boyfriend?" Shell asked.

"Uh, yeah."

Shell put on a big smile and stuck out his hand, walking over to Alan. "Pleased to meet you, Alan. Shell Compton. Officer Streng is going to be working undercover in my business."

Alan shook Shell's hand, but he looked somewhere between wary and angry. "And by undercover, you mean she has to have her shirt off?"

113

I looked down at my blouse. I'd undone the first three buttons, and somehow Shell had managed to remove the last few. I buttoned up, wondering how in the hell I was going to explain this.

"I run an escort service," Shell said. "Someone is murdering my girls. Officer Streng is going to pretend to work for me, to try to find the killer. I needed to take some sexy pics of her for her portfolio. That's how my clients pick their dates."

"Three women have died so far," I quickly added. "The files are on the kitchen counter."

"I see," Alan said, though he didn't sound very convinced.

"Are we done?" I asked Shell, though it was more a statement than a question.

"Yeah. Let me pack up my lights and—"

"I can do it and bring them tomorrow morning."

Shell nodded. "Sure thing. See you later. Good meeting you, Alan." Shell stepped around him, then let himself out.

"That was weird," Alan said. "Nothing like walking in on your girlfriend with another guy and her shirt off."

"My shirt was on," I said. "It was just open. Are those for me?"

Alan held out the flowers. I took the bouquet, gave it the perfunctory sniff, and engaged in an awkward hug with my boyfriend. I still was jittery from the shock of him showing up and surprising me, and wasn't sure what I was actually feeling. After all, Alan had never said *I love you*, and he'd completely forgotten my birthday.

"Happy birthday," Alan said. "I love you."

Whoa. He loved me? How was I supposed to respond to that? Say it back? Did I even want to?

Instead of responding in kind, I held Alan at an arm's length and searched his eyes. "My, uh, birthday was yesterday."

"You're kidding, right?" Alan said. "I wrote it down. It was this Tuesday."

"Today is Wednesday."

His face pinched. "Oh, geez, Jacqueline. I'm so sorry."

"It's okay," I said, even though it really wasn't. "At least now I know why you didn't call."

"Did you do anything special at least?"

"I did a prostitution sting and found a dismembered woman in a Dumpster."

"Fun. Was there birthday cake?"

I smiled, relaxing a notch. "No, there wasn't."

"I missed you."

"Missed you, too."

But did I? If I really did miss Alan, why was I playing tonsil tennis with some other guy?

"I know I've been kind of...distant...lately," he said, hooding his eyes. "The fact is, I've been thinking a lot. About us."

"And what have you been thinking about?"

Alan crouched down, like he was tying his shoe.

But he wasn't tying his shoe.

He was kneeling.

And he had a small, black box in his hand.

"I've been looking a long time for a woman like you, Jacqueline. I love being with you, and when we're apart, I think about you."

Oh my God. Oh my God oh my God oh my God. He was—

"Jacqueline Streng." Alan opened up the tiny box and took out the gold ring with the diamond in it. "Would you make me the happiest guy in the world and marry me?"

Present day
2010, August 10

I was having a horrible nightmare where I was tied up and someone was going to torture me to death. So there was no feeling of relief when I woke up and realized I was tied up and someone was going to torture me to death.

The Catherine Wheel, with its horrible Guinea Worm attachment, whirred in my vision, and next to it the digital clock continued its countdown.

1:40:26...1:40:25...1:40:24...

It reminded me of a case I had a few years ago. Another countdown, on a digital watch.

I hoped this one would end better than that one had.

My brain was still fuzzy, and I couldn't remember what had led up to this point. I also had no idea how I'd get out of this. If I didn't know where I was, how could anyone else?

I scooted backward, peering behind me, eyeing the concrete block I was tethered to. Then I looked at my burning wrists. There was blood, but not as much as I'd expected, and the pain was far out of proportion with the actual damage. The

116

wounds were no more than bad scrapes, but the glistening salt crystals made every millimeter of exposed flesh scream.

Unfortunately, the damage I'd done to the rope was even less impressive than the damage I'd done to myself. For all of my hard work, the nylon cord was barely frayed.

But seeing the Catherine Wheel had steeled my resolve. If I had to saw off both of my hands to get free, I would.

I closed my eyes and began to rub the rope against the corner of the block, whimpering in my throat, biting the ball gag so hard my jaw trembled.

Three years ago
2007, August 8

I hung up my cell phone and watched the cab pull up. Dalton and his associates climbed in. Good old Herb had slashed the tires of Dalton's Caddy and the Benz, based on my not-so-subtle suggestion, in an effort to keep them on the scene and buy some time while I called Libby Hellmann, the state's attorney.

Our efforts had bought us five minutes, and they were for naught. Hellmann had agreed with my original assessment; we had absolutely no evidence, and no probable cause, which meant we couldn't get paper on Dalton. No search warrant. No arrest.

Deep down, I knew Dalton had a child in a storage locker somewhere. A child who was running out of time. And there wasn't anything I could do. Even if I'd tried the loose-wire/vigilante-cop route and attempted to beat a confession out of Dalton, his lawyers showing up had squelched that plan. Not that it was ever a plan to begin with. I was pragmatic about following rules when confronted by a greater good, but unlike Mr. K I had no stomach for hurting people.

The only minor victory we scored was the look on the lawyer's face when he saw the flat tires. When he went up to Herb, spouting off about suing and calling superiors, my partner told them a story about a roving band of tire-slashing thugs who had a vendetta against luxury cars, which was why my Nova was spared. When asked why he didn't do anything to stop it, Herb replied, "I asked my lawyer, and he advised me not to."

I truly did love the man, in that brotherly/sisterly way.

"Follow the cab?" he asked. "Or break into his car?"

I considered it. On one hand, if we chased Dalton, he surely wouldn't lead us anywhere helpful. On the other, he wouldn't leave his car with us if there was anything important or incriminating in it. But we couldn't afford to miss that chance.

"Both," I decided. "Hurry up. There's a lock pick in my trunk."

I hit the button and Herb gracelessly extracted himself from my vehicle, pulling out my lock pick—a one gallon plastic milk jug filled with concrete—just as the cab was pulling away. I took off after Dalton, then pressed the button on my earpiece to keep in touch with Herb. After two rings, he picked up.

"Ms. Daniels, I hate to be the bearer of bad news, but I think this milk has gone bad."

"It's gone very bad," I said, smirking. "You may have to arrest it for B&E. Call me back if you find anything. I can have a car pick you up."

I heard the *CRUNCH* of breaking safety glass, and the whine of the car alarm. I killed the phone, then used the radio mic to call Tom Mankowski, the detective on my team.

"Car five-five-niner, this is Lewis."

Roy Lewis was Tom's partner. "Hey, Roy, it's Jack Daniels. Tom keeping you in the loop?"

"He don't tell me shit. Plus the dude's drunk all the time, on the take, and dealing crack to underprivileged schoolchildren. Plus he has erectile dysfunction."

I heard Tom say "asshole" in the background, then, "What's up, Lieut? I haven't confirmed Dalton's property in Cape Verde, but I did find his flight. He's taking United out of O'Hare on August ninth, two fifteen p.m."

I checked the current time, and the digital watch countdown. That coincided exactly with the time running out.

"I need you to arrange for a round-the-clock on John Dalton, sixty-one years of age, residing at 1300 North Lake Shore Drive. Three teams, eight-hour shifts."

"Roger that. Where is the suspect now?"

"In a yellow cab, just turned off of Clybourn, heading west on Diversey. I also need you to assemble a team and start calling every self-storage facility in Chicago, checking to see who's renting unit 515. If it's John Dalton, John Smith, John Doe, or anything cute, get me immediately. I'll be in touch. Out."

I cut off, then called home base. "Dispatch, this is Lieutenant Daniels out of the two-six. I need a car to rendezvous with me en route." I gave them my make, model, and plate number, as well as the upcoming intersection. Less than a minute later, a black-and-white pulled up alongside me. I read their car number off their front fender and got them on the mic.

"Car seven-six-three-seven, I need a photo taken to Scott Hajek at the crime lab. Complete workup, plus run the pic through missing persons. Grab it at the next stop."

We all came to a red light at Western, Dalton's cab right ahead of me, the patrol car on my side. A uniform—a young black woman who couldn't have been older than twenty-one—hopped out of the passenger seat and hurried to my window as I lowered it.

"It's really an honor to meet you, Lieutenant."

I checked her nametag. *Graves.* "Thanks for the assist, Officer Graves. I need this at the lab ASAP. Hit the lights."

"Roger that, Lieutenant." Graves held out an evidence bag, and I dropped the envelope inside. Before she ran off, Graves hesitated.

"Did you need something, Officer?"

"I just wanted to say I've been following your career since I was a little girl. You're the reason I became a cop, Lieutenant."

I was flattered, of course, but I played the hard-ass like I was supposed to. "Don't blame me for your unhappiness, Officer. Now move it or I'll have you busted down to traffic duty."

Her smile was sudden and dazzling. "Yes, ma'am," she said, then nodded and ran back to her patrol car. I wondered if I was ever that young and eager, anxious to make my mark, and decided I couldn't have been. The light turned green, and I followed the cab up to a club called Spill, which I knew from a case I had a long time ago. It was a known Outfit property, and it reminded me of a man I remembered from my early days in Homicide, a former mob enforcer.

I double-parked and watch the trio exit the cab. Dalton waved at me before going inside. My earpiece rang, and I picked up.

"Daniels."

"Car was clean, Jack. Not even an owner's manual in the glove compartment."

"I'm at Spill, Herb. Up for a shot of tequila?"

"I don't think I'm ready for tequila yet. But a beer would work."

"Need a ride?"

"I'll cab it."

"See you in a bit."

I hung up, parked in front of a hydrant, and headed into Chicago's biggest mob bar to see what trouble I could cause.

Present day
2010, August 10

Phin's nerves hummed throughout his body, making his extremities tingle and twitch. He was anxious to act, to do something, anything, to find Jack. But he had no idea what to do. Herb had taken the Lemonheads boxes, and the single yellow piece of candy stuck in the bough of the tree, and was trying to find latent prints on them. Harry was on his laptop, using Identi-Kit facial composite software to put together a picture of the creepy looking guy with the black hair who'd been hanging around his office.

Phin had nothing to do other than pace. He kept clenching and unclenching his fists, wanting to hit somebody. He checked on McGlade, half-expecting the uncouth private eye to be surfing porno, but found him working diligently on creating the composite. Then Phin checked on Herb in the kitchen, who was using a ninhydrin spray to stain the prints on the box and candy. It smelled like acetone, and Herb was working on the stove with the vent on.

Harry had checked the two unknown numbers on Jack's cell phone. Both were billing follow-ups for cases they'd recently had.

Phin considered calling Mary, Jack's mother, who was on yet another cruise—she took several a year. But Phin couldn't see any reason to ruin the old woman's trip, when there was nothing she'd be able to do to help.

"Got a bunch," Herb said, stepping away from the stove and fanning the air with his palm. "Some good ones. But they'll need to dry before I can lift them."

"Can you search the CPD database by arresting officer?" Phin asked.

"Sure. But Jack was on the force for more than twenty years. There are going to be over a thousand perps she arrested during that time."

Phin stared at Herb, hard. "Then we'd better get started."

Twenty-one years ago
1989, August 16

I looked at Alan, on one knee. Looked at the ring, a nice-size, round diamond. Looked back at Alan. Then at the ring. Then Alan. Then the ring.

"You're supposed to answer yes or no," Alan said. His eyes were bright, his face earnest and hopeful.

"Alan…I…well, I'm kind of blown away right now."

Alan waited.

"I mean, we've only been dating for a few months," I went on. "We haven't even lived together."

"I'm an old-fashioned guy. The time to live together is when we're engaged."

"Shouldn't living together come first? What if we can't stand being around each other all the time?"

Alan lost a bit of his sparkle. He closed the ring box and stood up. "You're going to be thirty next year. If we want to start a family, it has to be soon."

"I don't think I'm ready to have kids, Alan. That can happen later. My career—"

"Your career? A guy was just in your living room, taking pictures of you with your shirt off. That's the career you want?"

"It's not like that," I said. "This is what I've been working for, Alan. You know it's my goal to be a lieutenant—"

"—before you're forty. I know that, Jacqueline. But whenever you talk about your job, all I hear is how little respect you get, how they're holding you back, how no men want to work with you except that shithead Henry—"

"Harry."

"—because it's all a big, sexist old boys' network."

I put my hands on my hips. "This is my dream, Alan."

"And what about kids? Let's say you do get your dream job. Are you going to quit, at the height of your career, and drop everything to have babies?"

"I haven't thought that far ahead. I'm not saying I don't want to have a family. I'm saying I don't think I'm ready for one right now."

Alan shook his head, giving me one of his patented looks of disapproval. "You want to be forty-five and pregnant? By the time the kid is in college, you'll be in a nursing home."

"Of course not. I don't want children when I'm that old."

"Yesterday was your birthday. In three hundred and sixty-four days you'll have another one. You can be married and maybe pregnant by then, or working some other hooker sting for a bunch of chauvinists who don't respect you."

Alan stuck the ring in his pocket and headed for the door.

"Where are you going?" I asked.

"I'm not going to start an argument trying to convince you to marry me. Either you want to, or you don't. I love you, and I respect that you need some time to think. You're a fantastic, wonderful woman, and I know you'll make a terrific wife, and mother. But only if you're ready."

I didn't know if I was ready.

"Stay," I said. What I left unsaid was, *convince me this is the right thing to do.*

"I can't make this decision for you, Jacqueline. I know I'm ready. Most people our age are ready. Every single one of my friends is married."

"So you want to get married because all of your friends are?"

"I want to get married because I love you. But the clock is ticking. For both of us."

Alan reached the door, paused for a moment, then left. I considered going after him, but he was right. I did need to think about this.

I always assumed I'd get married and have children someday, but never really stopped to think how that would fit with my career. How could I rise up in the ranks if I needed to take a year off for maternity leave? How seriously would I be taken by the brass if I had to interrupt a high-profile murder investigation so I could stay home with my kid who had the chicken pox?

But, by the same token, I was almost thirty. I needed to make this decision, and soon. The fact was, if I didn't take this chance with Alan, I might never have another one.

Alan was right. The clock was ticking.

And boy, did I hate ticking clocks.

Three years ago
2007, August 8

With the clock ticking down on the unknown boy's life, I walked into Spill, wondering what more I could do to find him. My mind was filled with awful scenarios of what would happen when the timer reached zero. Was the boy in a storage locker in some sort of sealed container, with his air running out? Or maybe some terrible machine would turn on automatically, bringing death? Or did he have a rope around his neck, standing on a slowly melting block of ice?

I shook my head, forcing away the images, and stepped into the club. It used to be *the* nightspot in the city, trendy and hip and A-list. A lot had changed since the last time I'd been in here. Gone were the smoke and the thumping house music and the line around the block. Spill had gone from popular to passé, the dance floor covered with a few lonely pool tables, the once-mighty bar reduced to serving fried pub grub and boilermakers to aging wiseguys. That's where I found Dalton and his lawyer cronies, sitting on stools at the bar. I parked myself at the other end, watching them glance at me and then huddle in private conversation.

Okay, Jack. You're here. Now what?

I ordered an orange juice, playing out various possibilities. As long as Dalton was kept under surveillance, we could arrest him once we had enough evidence to satisfy probable cause.

The term *probable cause* was misused a lot on TV shows and in books. In U.S. law, it meant a cop could only arrest a suspect if there was information sufficient to convince the cop that a perp had committed a crime, or that evidence of a crime or contraband would be found if a search was conducted. This would justify a search warrant or an arrest warrant, and it had to be able to stand up in court, at a probable cause hearing.

I had a reasonable suspicion that Dalton had abducted a child, and was possibly the enigmatic Mr. K. As a law enforcement officer, that allowed me to detain Dalton for brief periods to question him, and search him if I suspected he had a weapon on him. But it didn't allow me to bring him in. All he'd given me was double-talk and innuendo, and the case would get kicked before even making it to the arraignment. Even if I perjured myself, lying to the judge and testifying that Dalton had said or done things he really hadn't, I'd still be required to prove those things at the hearing. The fact that Dalton had survived this long without a single blemish on his record showed he was unlikely to make mistakes, and having his lawyers meet him at the storage area was smart. I couldn't get to him, either legally or illegally.

Herb walked in, pulling up a stool next to me.

"I left the key under your car," he said, referring to the concrete milk jug. "Anything happening?"

"Nothing so far. The guy is leaving the country tomorrow, and is possibly about to murder a child, and he's sitting there without a care in the world."

Herb picked up the plastic table tent that served as a menu. "Hmm. They have batter-fried bacon."

I frowned at him. "Wouldn't it be faster just to inject the cholesterol directly into your arteries?"

"Probably not. Doesn't matter, though. As of right now, I'm officially on a diet. It was pretty embarrassing not being able to sit up in your car."

"Good for you," I said.

The bartender came back, and Herb ordered some fried zucchini sticks. When I gave him the stink eye, Herb said, "What? They're vegetables."

I turned my attention back to Dalton. If one of the leads panned out, we could grab him. But I couldn't count on that. If he really was Mr. K, I couldn't let him leave the country. It violated everything I stood for.

So how could I make him stay?

"If we saw him committing a crime, we could arrest him," Herb said. My partner often seemed able to read my mind.

"What are you thinking?" I asked.

"We could plant drugs on him."

"Drugs?"

"I saw that on *The Shield*."

"Good idea. Give me that bag of cocaine you always carry around with you."

Herb frowned. "Maybe I could get some out of the evidence locker."

"You'd have to sign for it. Internal Affairs would love that."

"Don't you know any dealers we could shake down?" he asked.

"No. You?"

"No. We're not very good crooked cops."

Both Herb and I knew this was fantasy talk, not real. While we'd both bent a few rules in our days, planting evidence just wasn't going to happen.

"I could try to provoke him into taking a swing at me," Herb said.

"Dalton wouldn't do it. And if you tried it in front of his lawyers, you'd be facing a harassment lawsuit."

But that got me thinking. I pulled out my cell.

"Who are you calling?" Herb asked.

"We're cops. Our hands are tied. What we need is help from someone who isn't so encumbered by the law."

"Jack, you're not really considering..."

He picked up on the first ring. "Hiya, Jackie. Is this a booty call? I think I can squeeze you in tonight. When you stop by, wear something slutty. And bring a pizza."

I rolled my eyes. "That isn't going to happen. But I do need your help."

"I like needy women."

"I'm at Spill. Get over here as fast as you can, Harry."

Present day
2010, August 10

I had to stop rubbing my wrists against the concrete because I was crying again. It was both shocking and disheartening how a little salt on some superficial wounds hurt so much. I blew air out of my nose, clearing my nasal passages, trying once more to get my breathing under control. The countdown clock drew my eyes yet again.

1:12:19...1:12:18...

I peered over my shoulder, looking to see the amount of nylon cord I'd managed to cut through, feeling a surge of panic when I saw I hadn't even gotten a third of the way through one of the ropes, and my wrists were wound around several times.

Doing a quick mental calculation, I realized I wasn't going to free myself in time. I had to speed this up, or I would still be tied up when the clock reached zero.

Snorting in a big, wet breath, my eyes blurry with tears, I sawed my burning wrists against the concrete with renewed fervor brought about by raw fear. My salted wounds hurt more than just about anything I'd ever felt.

But I knew the Catherine Wheel would be a lot worse.

Twenty-one years ago
1989, August 17

Everyone kept staring at me when I got to the office that morning. No one said anything to my face, or even made direct eye contact. But I kept catching sideways glances and seeing whispered exchanges, to the point where I was feeling sort of paranoid. I wondered if I had my Armani suit on backwards, or toilet paper stuck to my shoe. A quick mirror check in the restroom didn't answer any questions for me; I thought I looked fine.

I'd been to the third floor, Homicide, only a few times. It was a large area, the desks all out in the open. After weaving through a few aisles, I found Detective Herb Benedict pecking away at a keyboard and squinting into a green monochrome monitor. Next to him was a box of a dozen donuts, half of them missing. Like Shell, I had no idea where Herb put those extra calories. But I was more impressed by his computer. That he had his own, rather than had to share it, meant he must have been more important than I'd guessed. Those things cost more than my car.

Herb looked up at me, raising an eyebrow. "May I help you, ma'am?"

I set the files I was holding—the prior victims—on his desk. "Reporting for duty, Detective."

He seemed puzzled, and then his eyes went wide.

"Jacqueline? Uh...wow. I actually didn't recognize you. That's some suit."

"Thanks." I didn't mention Shell bought it, having no idea if that violated some sort of ethics code or rule. "Nice computer."

Herb smiled. "Thanks. Can you believe it has twenty megabytes of memory?"

"That's insane," I said, shaking my head. "Who would ever need that much?"

"The world is changing so fast I can't even keep up. Do you know what a cellular radio phone is?"

"Those big, clunky portable things that look like bricks with huge antennas? Like Michael Douglas used in *Wall Street*?"

Herb nodded. "They sell for a cool four grand. But I heard they're working on making them more affordable. Technology experts predict one out of a thousand people will have a cell phone by the year twenty-ten."

"In just twenty years? No way. I can't even imagine needing one. And it's not like I could fit that giant thing in my purse."

"Maybe they'll get smaller," Herb said. He leaned back, lacing his fingers behind his head. "Did you review the vics' files?"

I nodded. I'd been up late last night, poring over the files. The three victims had all died in similar fashions, of internal bleeding. All had been drugged, and dismembered. All had been found in Dumpsters, without heads. Alongside one of the bodies was a bloody ball gag. That last detail popped out at me. I remembered that lecture from the police academy, about Unknown Subject K.

"Have you ever encountered a victim where a ball gag was used?" I asked.

Herb's eyes twinkled. "You're thinking about Mr. K, aren't you?"

"It's one of his signatures."

"Possible. It's also possible all the unsolveds that involved gags are being incorrectly lumped together and attributed to some imaginary boogeyman."

"Is that what you think?"

"I like keeping an open mind. I find that if I pursue an investigation with a bias, I might miss something important because it doesn't fit with my theory. Ready to visit Shell's office?"

"Yeah."

Herb let me drive, which blew my mind. In my time on patrol, and being partners with McGlade, I never drove. Perhaps Herb was confident enough that it didn't bother him to let a woman take control. Or perhaps he was just lazy.

"A Chevy Nova," Herb said, sliding into the passenger seat. "Nice. Roomy, too."

"I figure I'll keep it another year, then trade up to something nicer. Where we headed?"

"River North. Rush and Ohio."

I pulled out of the police parking lot and melded into traffic. For August, it was cooler than normal. There was still the muggy humidity from being close to Lake Michigan, but it wasn't devastating my hair and makeup like it normally did this time of year.

"So what other thoughts did you have, looking at the files?" Herb said.

"All three of the victims went on dates with two of the same men. Both older. Both rich, without records."

"Would you consider them suspects?"

"No." I smiled at Herb. "But I like to keep an open mind."

"Any link among the women?"

"They were all escorts. Two were white, one was of Asian descent. All three were very pretty. Two were college-educated, and the third was working on her bachelor's degree, part- time. And all three earned more per year than I do. Plus there was something else I found interesting."

"What's that?"

I turned onto Michigan, hitting the gas. The car was a bit sluggish—one of the reasons I was going to replace it soon. "The girl who didn't work for Shell worked for a company called Elite Escorts. It's a small operation, just a dozen girls. Like Shell's. I called a few other services last night, and most of them are big. Fifty, a hundred girls. The Dodd Agency—the one Shell said has been aggressively pursuing his girls—is one of the biggies."

"Why would they be involved? They're a big fish. Shell is a small fry."

"Don't you know your Darwin?" I asked. "The big fish eat the small ones. That's how they get big."

Michigan Avenue was stop-and-go, crammed with people in cars and on foot. This area was quintessential Chicago to me. Shops and hotels. Further ahead, the Art Institute, Grant Park, the Buckingham Fountain, the Field Museum, Shedd Aquarium, Adler Planetarium. Soldier Field, where the Bears played. The Magnificent Mile, with beaches and one of the most memorable city skylines in the world. My kind of town, and the reason I would never ever move to the suburbs.

There wasn't a single place to park on Michigan, even illegally, so we looped up to Grand, turned right, and got onto Rush.

"Turn in the alley, here. Shell said we can park around back."

Herb directed me into a little three-car lot behind the buildings, two spots already taken with a Cadillac and a black Honda.

I pulled in and stepped out into the alley, smoothed my pants, adjusted my shoulder pads, and picked up Shell's box of lights and his backdrop. Herb took the box from me.

"Yuck," he said, making a face. The garbage smell was bad enough to melt my eyeballs. I held a hand over my nose and mouth, and we hurried out onto Rush Street.

Together we walked past Pizzeria Uno—where deep-dish pizza was invented back in the 1950s—up to a small boutique-style building shared by an art gallery and Classy Companions, Shell's agency. After climbing the concrete steps and entering the enclosed porch through a door on spring hinges, we were slapped by a blast of frigid air. The buzzers along the security door had options for the two businesses, and several tenants living above them.

"Other people live in the building," I said to Herb, thinking I hadn't seen anything about tenants in the reports. Statistics showed that over ninety percent of murders were committed by someone who knew the victim.

"Women. All of Shell's ladies," Herb said, pressing the buzzer. "This is where you'll be staying for the duration of the case."

After a moment, the speaker above the buzzers said, "Classy Companions." It was a female voice, deep and husky.

"Detective Herb Benedict, and Officer Jacqueline Streng," Herb answered.

The door buzzed, and we went in. The hallway divided the bottom floor into two halves. On one side was the gallery, on the other, the agency. The door to Classy Companions was heavy wood, the company name stenciled on at eye-level. Herb pointed over our heads and I looked up, seeing the security camera.

"Is that new?" I asked.

"Shell put it in after the first murder."

"You've reviewed all the tapes?"

"Yeah. There will be a VCR in your room for you to review them as well."

Herb knocked, and again we needed to be buzzed in. The lobby was plush, all pastels and soft lighting. The carpet was so thick my heels sank into it. I saw a few sofas and loveseats, a waiting area boasting a coffee table piled with magazines, assorted floor plants, and a stunning fresh flower arrangement on the front desk that reminded me of the flowers Alan had given me last night when he proposed—flowers I'd forgotten to put in a vase.

The woman behind the desk was old, in her forties, graying and plump. Her makeup was expertly applied, and she already had a smile on, anticipating our approach.

"Hello, Detective." When she looked at me, her wattage went down a notch, but most of the smile stayed. "And you must be Jacqueline. That's the same outfit as in your pictures."

I forced a polite grin. "Nice to meet you, Mrs....?"

"Mizz," she corrected, "Elizabeth White. Everyone here calls me Mizz Lizzy." She picked up a pink phone on her desk and hit a button. "Mr. Compton? Detective Benedict and the woman are here."

Mizz Lizzy didn't try to engage us in further conversation, instead burying her nose in a Rolodex. I'd been around enough catty women to apply the adjective to her. She either didn't like cops, or didn't like me.

After a minute of Herb and I staring at each other, Shell entered. He was wearing a different tailored suit than the night before, and he looked terrific, approaching with a big grin, taking the lighting box from Herb and the backdrop from me.

"Good morning, Herb, Jacqueline. Did Mizz Lizzy offer you coffee?"

"I'd love a cup," I said. I really wasn't a big coffee drinker, but I liked the idea of the older woman serving me.

"Cream and sugar?" she asked.

"Black."

"Anything for you, Detective?"

"Black coffee sounds great," Herb replied.

Mizz Lizzy swiveled out from behind her desk and waddled off into another room. Shell set down the equipment and beamed at me. "You look terrific. I hope you're up for a long day, because we've already booked you twice. You have a lunch date with Felix Sarcotti, and dinner and the theater tonight with Jeroen ten Berge."

I recognized the two names from the victims' files. Both men had dated all three of the deceased.

"That was fast," I said. "They saw my picture already?"

"They're both longtime clients, and insist on seeing any new girl as soon as she comes in. I messengered your photos to them this morning, and they're both eager to meet you. But we have much to do before lunch. We need to get started right away. Mizz Lizzy!" Shell called into the other room. "Bring the coffee up to Sandy's room, if you would!"

Shell put his hands lightly on my arms, his face bright and enthusiastic. "You're going to like Sandy, I think. She's really fascinating. She's also had a...shall we say...*checkered past*."

"A police record?" I asked.

"No. She was never actually charged with a crime."

I looked at Herb, confused. His eyes bored into mine. "Sandy Sechrest, twenty-five years old. Four years ago she killed a man."

Present day
2010, August 10

"How about this guy?" Phin called out while squinting at the computer. For the past half hour, he and Herb had been looking at Jack's arrest record, cross-referencing perps' names on the World Wide Web to see if anything recent or interesting came up. They'd gotten as far as the Bs, then Herb waddled off to check if the ninhydrin had dried.

"What's Jack's network password?" Harry asked, walking into the room. "I need to print my guy out."

"It's *crimefighter*."

"Lame," Harry said, leaning over Phin's shoulder. "Who's that fugly bastard?"

"His name is Victor Brotsky."

Brotsky was fifty-eight years old, pudgy, sweaty, unshaven, with a lazy eye that made him look even crazier than his police record proved he was. The reason Phin was interested in him was twofold. First, he'd recently been denied parole, and rightfully so—the guy was a butcher. The second was an article from three months ago that appeared in the *Chicago Record* written by someone named Alex Chapa, which showed up in a Google search. *SERIAL KILLER DONATES $50K TO CHARITY.*

"What's up?" Herb said, coming into the room.

"Remember this guy?" Phin asked, zooming in on the article.

Herb squinted at the reporter's picture. "Chapa? Yeah, we crossed paths a few times. A bit of a pain in the ass, but he wouldn't do anything to Jack."

"Not him. Victor Brotsky."

"Oh, yeah," Herb nodded, his chins jiggling. "The worst of the worst."

"In May he donated fifty thousand bucks to Children's Memorial Hospital," Phin said. "Apparently, a rich relative of his died in Russia, leaving him a ton of money."

"So he tried to buy himself a parole," Herb said. "And when that didn't work, maybe he hired a hit man to go after the one who arrested him."

"Would he be the type to do that?"

"Brotsky? He was an animal. He had to be in restraints during his trial because he tried to attack Jack while she was on the stand."

Phin scrolled down, scanning the article. "He's in Stateville. About an hour drive. We can keep searching for other possibles on Jack and Harry's laptops while we're driving. Do you have connections at the prison, Herb?"

Herb shook his head.

"I do," McGlade said. "I know the warden. Guy named Miller. He owes me one. We were at a strip club, and he was heading to the champagne room with a hottie until I pointed out her Adam's apple. I'll give him a call." He looked at Herb. "We could use the law on our side to talk to Brotsky and search his cell. You might have to throw your weight around."

141

Herb folded his arms and frowned.

"What?" Harry said.

"I'm waiting for the insult."

"No insult. If the superintendant is behind this, it'll make it easier."

Herb nodded. "Okay. Let me fax the Lemonheads box to the crime lab."

"I'll give you my Indenti-Kit composite, too," Harry said.

Phin was surprised. He didn't expect the two of them to actually be able to work together. Perhaps they understood the urgency of the situation and were able to put aside their mutual hate society and act like reasonable adults.

Both Harry and Herb took off. A minute later, the printer began to hum, spitting out computer-generated pictures of the man McGlade had seen outside his office, both head-on and profile. Long black hair. Vacant eyes. A pointy chin. Creepy looking guy.

The next pictures were even creepier. Harry had taken Herb's head and Photoshopped it onto a walrus, with an erection. Subsequent pics had the Herb/walrus apparently making love to various famous people, both male and female. The one that had Herb being ridden by Hitler was particularly well done, for what it was.

In the interest of diplomacy, Phin threw them away before Herb returned with the Lemonheads candy box. It took two minutes to make scans of all six cardboard sides, the prints showing up as purple ink. As Herb was e-mailing them, Harry came back in.

"Did my pics print?" he asked.

Phin handed over the two of the long-haired man.

"How about the others?" Harry asked.

"That was it, McGlade."

Harry bent down, studying the printer. "You didn't see one with the Skipper from *Gilligan's Island?*"

Phin saw it, and wished there was some way he could *unsee* it. He grabbed the keys to Jack's SUV. "Let's move," he said.

But the small amount of optimism he had was waning. If Brotsky had hired someone to abduct Jack, it was unlikely he'd talk. And how do you threaten or bargain with a guy who was going to spend the rest of his days locked in a maximum security prison?

Three years ago
2007, August 8

McGlade strolled into Spill and spotted us immediately. "Hiya, Jackie." He glanced at Herb. "Jabba. How's the rest of the Hutt? Fat and ugly?"

I put a firm hand on Herb's shoulder, holding him in his seat.

"We need your help, Harry," I said.

"To roll El Chubbo out of here? We'll need a few more guys, and a block and tackle."

"Remember Mr. K?" I asked.

"The breakfast cereal?"

Herb leered at Harry. "Did you get in line for seconds when God was handing out the stupid?" he asked.

"Did you get in line for seconds when God was handing out the sweet potatoes?"

"Enough," I said. "The older guy sitting further down the bar. We think he might have abducted a child, but we've got nothing on him. We want you to provoke him enough so he takes a swing at you, so we can arrest him."

"Shouldn't take you more than a few seconds," Herb said.

Harry glanced over his shoulder. Dalton and his two lawyers were looking at us.

"What's in this for me?" Harry asked.

"You'd be saving a young boy's life," Herb said.

"So that's worth, what, in U.S. dollars?" He winked at me. "Or sexual favors?"

Herb jerked his thumb at Harry. "How about I beat him up, and we say it was Dalton?" he said.

"Settle down there, Humpty. I'm just messing with you. Except for the money part. You'll be getting my invoice in the mail."

Herb and I moved closer as Harry marched over to their part of the bar. "Which one of you assholes is Special K?"

"I know you," Dalton said. "You're that private eye, Harrison Harold McGlade. There's a TV show about you."

"*Fatal Autonomy*," Harry said, nodding. "You a fan?"

"A big fan. Could I get your autograph?"

"Sure!"

Dalton passed over a napkin, and Harry pulled out a pen and began to sign it. Next to me, I heard Herb slap himself in the forehead.

"So what's all this I hear about a child abduction?" Harry asked.

Dalton kept his face neutral. "I have no idea what you're talking about."

"Don't you threaten me!" Harry yelled.

"Excuse me? I'm not threatening you."

In a quick move, Harry grabbed Dalton by the lapels and yanked him out of his chair. McGlade fell backwards, Dalton landing on top of him.

"Get off of me!" Harry yelled. "Police! I need the police! I'm being assaulted!"

I winced. This hadn't played out as I'd hoped. But then, what could I have honestly been hoping for?

"Are there any fat cops in the bar!" Harry wailed.

"On the bright side," Herb said, "Dalton's lawyers will no doubt press charges, and with any luck McGlade will go to jail for a few years."

I walked over there before it got any worse. "Get up, McGlade," I ordered him.

"A cop! Thank heavens! This man is attempting murder!"

Harry was pulling Dalton's hand toward his own throat. It didn't quite reach, but McGlade still made choking noises and puffed out his cheeks like he was being strangled. I reached down, pulled Dalton free, and then knelt on Harry's stomach.

"Are you high?" I said through clenched teeth.

"A little."

The lawyers began to shout at me, hurling legal terms like *harassment* and *battery* and *litigation*. Dalton, for his part, looked slightly bemused. I decided to try to turn this lemon into lemonade.

"Mr. Dalton," I said, "I saw the whole thing. I suggest you come down to the station and press charges."

"What?!" McGlade shouted.

Herb bent over next to Harry. "You have the right to remain silent," he said, a terse grin on his face, as he snapped a cuff on McGlade's wrist. "Which I heartily endorse."

Dalton smoothed his hands over his suit. "I won't be pressing charges. I simply don't have the time." He stared over at me. "Time is such a precious thing, isn't it, Jack? We really should savor every minute. Some of us only have so long left."

Herb and I hefted McGlade up to his feet.

"I'll be seeing you," I told Dalton.

"No you won't. But maybe I'll call you later, after I land."

We dragged Harry out of there. Once back on the street, McGlade said, "I think that went well. Can you get these cuffs off?" Neither Herb nor I made any effort to follow his request. "What's up? Why so lugubrious?"

"God, I hate him," Herb muttered to himself.

"Come on. You're not really arresting me. Are you?"

I sighed. "Herb, let him go."

"Do we have to?"

I nodded. My partner made a face, but freed Harry's wrists.

"What were you thinking?" I asked. "Don't you remember what it was like to be a cop? There's a child's life at stake here."

Harry rolled his eyes. "Jeez, Jackie. Gimme a little credit, will you? If that guy is Mr. K, he's as cold as they come. There was no way he'd lose his temper and throw a punch. Especially in front of two cops."

"So instead, you think it's helpful to make an ass out of yourself?" Herb said.

"No, Shamu. That was just a distraction." Harry reached into his pocket and held up something, his face triumphant. "Who wants to see that SOB's wallet?"

Present day
2010, August 10

When the countdown timer dropped under sixty minutes, I once again checked out the bindings around my wrists. Through blurry, tear-filled eyes, I saw I hadn't even gotten through half the rope.

It was no use. I wouldn't make it in time. My wrists hurt more than anything I'd ever felt before, like tiny fanged creatures were nibbling away at my raw skin. I let my head rest on the floor, wondering what I was supposed to do next.

Rather than look at the slowly spinning Catherine Wheel, I stared up at the ceiling of the storage locker. I wasn't a spiritual person. Not one bit. Even so, I searched my mind for any prayers I knew.

That's when I saw it. Something above me. Something that glinted as it moved.

I blinked away the wetness clouding my pupils, squinting at the object, quickly realizing what it was.

A camera. The son of a bitch was watching me.

Despair dropped on me like a cold, wet blanket. Even if I miraculously beat the countdown clock and untied myself, it wouldn't matter. If Mr. K was keeping an eye me, he would know when I was breaking free. No doubt he was close by, ready to come in at any moment.

And when that knowledge sank in, I realized, with chilling certainty, that there truly was no way out.

I was finished. This was the end. The only question remaining was how long it would take me to die.

Twenty-one years ago
1989, August 17

"It was deemed self-defense," Herb said. "Charges weren't filed."

We were discussing one of Shell's escorts, Sandy Sechrest, while climbing the carpeted stairs to the apartments where the women lived. As with the front door and the lobby, the stairwell had a locked security door.

"What were the particulars?" I asked.

"Live-in boyfriend," Herb said. "History of violence. Roughed her up, threatening to kill her. She stabbed him in the throat with a steak knife. Witnesses heard the incident through the apartment walls, and she had defensive wounds on her body indicative of abuse."

"This was just after Sandy joined the agency," Shell said. "That's when I decided the girls would be safest if they all lived under one roof. The security here is good. All of the doors are reinforced. The girls have to sign their visitors in. In each room there's also a panic button, directly linked to the building's burglar alarm system. No numbers on the apartments, so even if a stalker managed to get up here, he wouldn't know who lived where. I take the girls' safety very seriously."

The second floor hallway was tastefully furnished, the same as downstairs. The sconces on the stucco walls provided plenty of light, and the doors to the apartments all had deadbolts.

"Why no security cameras up here?" I asked.

"There's a fine line between safety and privacy," Shell said, knocking on the first door on the left. "Cameras would be a bit too intrusive."

The door opened, and a gorgeous brunette answered. Besides her classic Lauren Bacall looks, she also had bigger shoulder pads and hair than I did. I bit back the tinge of envy I was feeling.

"Sandy, you know Detective Benedict. I'd like you to meet our new girl, Jacqueline Streng."

Sandy smiled, but it was without warmth, and she didn't offer her hand. "Nice to meet you Jacqueline. I'm sure you'll fit in perfectly here." Her gaze flitted to Shell. "Shelly, my brunch date is picking me up at eleven, but won't be able to take me home. Can I cab it?"

"I'd prefer you call me for a ride."

She nodded. "I still have to get ready."

"We won't keep you, Sandy."

Sandy closed the door, and I heard the deadbolt snick into place.

"How many girls live here?" I asked.

"Eight. You'll make nine."

"Are they all that beautiful?" I asked.

Shell's eyes twinkled. "They are. That's why you're going to fit in perfectly here."

I was flattered by Shell's compliment, but it made me think of Alan. He hadn't said I was beautiful when he proposed to me last night. But was that a good thing or a bad thing? Did I want to be with a man who valued my looks more than my personality or intelligence? And if so, why did it make me feel so good to have someone comment on my appearance? Was I that shallow and vain?

The stairwell door swung open, and Mizz Lizzy appeared, carrying a silver tray with two cups of coffee. Without a word she handed one to me, and to Herb. I lifted the delicate, bone china cup and took a sip. Delicious.

"Thank you," I said.

Mizz Lizzy ignored me. "Anything else, Shell?"

"We're fine for the moment."

She curtseyed—something I hadn't seen done in person in quite a while—and then walked off. Shell led us to the next apartment. A blonde answered. A blonde with a perfect face and boobs that made Loni Anderson look like a man.

"Gloria, I don't believe you've met Detective Benedict. He's in charge of the investigation."

"I love your mustache, Detective." She batted her eyelashes, which were so long they had to be fake. "I love the feel of a man's facial hair on my thighs."

"You and me both," Herb said.

"And this is our new girl, Jacqueline Streng."

"Do you go by Jack?" Gloria asked. "My sister's name is Jacqueline, and we all call her Jack."

I shook my head. "No. I prefer Jacqueline."

"Too bad." Gloria pouted, as if I'd scolded her. "Are you into girls?"

"Excuse me?"

"You know. Bi?"

"Uh, no. I have a boyfriend."

"I've got plenty of boyfriends," Gloria giggled. And jig-gled. "But girls are nice, too."

"Even though I don't have a mustache?" I said.

Gloria gave me a gentle poke in the shoulder. "I like you. You're funny." She stuck out her lower lip at Shell. "Shelly, I thought you were supposed to come by this morning. Where were you?"

Shell turned to us. "Can you excuse me just a second?"

Without waiting for our response, he stepped inside Glo-ria's apartment.

"She looks like a *Playboy* model," I said.

Herb leaned back, talking to me softly out of the side of his mouth. "She's cute. But is she the district quick-draw champion?"

I suppressed a smile, but inside I was beaming. Being praised for my shooting skills felt a lot better than being called beautiful.

"Speaking of," Herb said. "Are you carrying right now?"

"Beretta, in my purse."

"Nine millimeter?"

"Three-eighty."

"Does it ever jam on you?" he asked.

"All semi-autos occasionally jam. But nothing I can't clear in a second or two."

"In the field, a second or two can be an eternity. I've got a .38 Colt, a Detective Special, I can loan you for this job."

"That only holds six rounds," I said. My Beretta held eight.

"But those six are guaranteed to fire."

"Thanks, but I'll stick with the semi."

Herb nodded. Though I had no romantic interest in Herb at all, I found myself glancing at his left hand. As I'd guessed, there was a wedding band. The good men were always already spoken for.

"Can I ask you a personal question, Herb?"

"As long as it doesn't involve my mustache."

"It doesn't. Do you like being married?"

"Absolutely," he said without hesitation. "Best thing I ever did in my life. You thinking about it?"

"My boyfriend proposed to me yesterday night." I wasn't sure why I was telling him this.

"Congratulations. What did you say?"

"I said I needed time. I have career goals, and I don't know if they'll fit with marriage."

"If he loves you," Herb said, "he'll respect your goals."

That's what I'd been thinking. But it was nice to hear it said aloud. "Did your wife, when you proposed, say she needed time?" I asked.

"She said yes before I even finished asking." He winked at me. "I think it was the mustache."

Maybe that's why I didn't say yes to Alan right away. He didn't have a mustache.

Gloria's door opened, and Shell popped out into the hallway. He had some lipstick on his neck that I was pretty sure wasn't there before.

"Ready to meet the rest of the girls?" he asked.

I nodded. But part of me wondered if maybe I was crazy for pursuing this whole cop thing. Maybe I'd be happier getting married and having kids.

And if that were the case, maybe Alan's proposal was my last shot at happiness.

Three years ago
2007, August 8

"Every time I think my opinion of you couldn't possibly get any lower, you pull a rabbit out of your hat," I told Harry.

"Or a perp's wallet out of his pants." He handed the aforementioned wallet to me. "I'll send you my bill in the mail. I'm saving up to buy a monkey."

Years ago, Harry had a fish tank. Not a single one survived. Hopefully a primate would fare better.

"Good luck with that," I told him.

"I think it would be fun to have a pet that could fetch me beer. Plus I could give him a tin cup, pretend to be blind, and make a few bucks on the L train."

"Quite the plan," Herb said.

"Yeah. But in total honesty, I'll probably just blow the money on malt liquor and lap dances."

"Thanks for your help, McGlade."

He nodded at me, gave Herb the finger, and walked off down the street. Every once in a while, McGlade came through for me. But I was incredibly grateful not to be working with him anymore. I couldn't imagine going down that route ever again.

155

I tapped Herb and we quickly got into my car, driving away before Dalton figured out Harry had ripped him off. Then I double-parked two streets over and examined our prize.

The wallet looked like any other men's wallet. Brown leather, trifold, worn in. Dalton had a Platinum American Express, a Visa bank card, and a driver's license in the various pockets. In the billfold compartment he had three hundred and forty dollars and a strip of paper with a twelve-digit number on it. There was a familiar logo in the corner.

"Federal Express," I said. "He FedExed something."

"Recently?" Herb said.

The paper was from an express U.S. airbill. Normally, it was attached to a full receipt that listed the sender and the recipient, along with a description of contents, packaging, and services. This had been torn off, so only the tracking number remained. It appeared new—things that were in wallets for a long time tended to have a faded, frayed look. The fold was still crisp. The colors still fine.

"I think so. Let's see."

Using my iPhone, I got online and accessed the FedEx Web site. Personally, I loved the iPhone, but part of me missed the good old days when phones had huge antennas and weighed two pounds.

"I ever tell you about the time a cell phone saved my life?" I asked Herb.

"About a million billion times."

"I think I need a new partner. Someone who appreciates my classic stories."

I used the touch screen to punch in the tracking number. It told me no information was available, indicating the package wasn't in their system yet.

"His condo," Herb said, snapping his fingers and pointing at me. "It had a FedEx box in the lobby."

I got on the radio and told Dispatch to send a car to Spill and keep an eye on John Dalton, filling in the particulars. Then Herb and I headed back to 1300 North Lake Shore Drive. Traffic seemed excruciatingly slow. I thought about calling the nearest squad car and having them check it out before we got there, but that involved all sorts of potential legal trouble. If Dalton had put something dangerous in the FedEx box, we'd need a warrant to take it. In order to get a warrant, we'd have to prove he put something in the box, and the only way we could prove that was with a receipt that we'd stolen. Better to just handle it ourselves.

I parked in front of Dalton's condo, hopped out of my Nova, and hurried up to the doorman.

"Has FedEx come yet?"

"Yeah."

"When?"

"About an hour ago."

Shit. "Do you know the driver? Know his name?"

"Naw. Different guy every time."

Double shit. I hurried back to the car just as Herb was pulling himself out. "Get in. We need to call FedEx, find out what truck the package is on."

After three minutes of navigating the plethora of phone tree options, I got a human being and explained that I was a cop in need of finding a package. After another ten minutes on hold, I was redirected to someone in authority. Rather than giving me a run-around, FedEx was surprisingly helpful. As soon as the tracking number was uploaded into the system—which should be within the next half hour—the local station would locate the package and wait for me to pick it up and take a look. No warrant, no judge, no hassle. Apparently, when you sent something FedEx, they could view the contents at their discretion if it was suspicious. A call from a police officer was enough to induce suspicion.

So Herb and I sat there, engine running, me refreshing the FedEx Web site every few minutes, waiting for the tracking number to be updated. When it finally was recognized by their system, I called the number they gave me, and they contacted the driver. I was able to speak to him directly.

"Got it right here, Officer." He had a nasally Chicago accent, pure South Side. "It's a small box, about two pounds. It dangerous?"

"I don't know," I said honestly. According to the Web, the package was set to be delivered tomorrow to a Chicago zip code. If it were a bomb, it probably wouldn't go off until it reached its destination. "Does it have an odor? Is it leaking?"

"Ask if it's ticking," Herb said. I shushed him.

"Seems like a normal package. If you want to come take a look, I'm on Division, in the Dominick's parking lot."

"We'll be there in five minutes," I said. "You might want to, uh, wait outside the truck. Maybe a few yards away. Who is the package addressed to?"

"Gotta be a fake," the driver said. "Is there any real person in the world actually named *Jack Daniels*?"

Present day
2010, August 10

"Oh...man."

"What is it, Harry?" Phin checked the rearview and stared at Harry, who was on the phone with the warden of Stateville Correctional Center. At Harry's prodding, and with a few calls from Herb's superiors, they'd placed Victor Brotsky in the isolation unit and had searched his cell.

"Brotsky had an iPhone hidden in his mattress," Harry said. He looked ashen. "There's some kind of live webcam video image on it. A woman tied up in a small room."

Phin squeezed the SUV's steering wheel hard enough for his forearms to shake. "Is it Jack?"

"Brunette, forties, hogtied with a gag in her mouth. Could be Jack."

"Is she...alive?" Phin asked, fighting to keep his voice steady.

Harry's face was slack. "Yeah. But there's a digital clock next to her. It's...counting down."

"How long?" whispered Herb.

"Less than thirty minutes."

Phin hit the gas. They were on Joliet Road, about eight miles away from the prison.

"Maybe it isn't her," Harry said.

Phin hoped that was the case. But he knew better. It wouldn't be the first time one of Jack's old cases had come back to haunt her. Imagining Jack tied up, in front of a camera, to be killed for some psycho's amusement, made Phin's stomach hurt worse than a year's worth of chemotherapy. In a way, though, it was better to know where Jack was than to not have a clue. When you know your enemy, you can fight your enemy.

"This Victor Brotsky," Phin said to Herb. "How bad was he?"

"The worst of the worst. If he's got Jack..." Herb's voice cracked.

But Victor Brotsky couldn't have Jack. He was locked up.

However, he might know who *did* have Jack.

And if he did, nothing on this planet could save Victor Brotsky from Phineas Troutt.

Twenty-one years ago
1989, August 17

After meeting the rest of the girls, then washing my hands in an attempt to wipe off some of the rampant neuroses that seemed to pervade Shell's escort agency like smoke damage, I went on my first official date with Felix Sarcotti.

Mr. Sarcotti was a wee bit older than God. His back was bent like a question mark, he walked with a black, silver-tipped cane, and his facial expression was a permanent leer.

He was also a perfect gentleman, and I had a great time accompanying him to lunch at the Signature Room, on the ninety-fifth floor of the John Hancock Building. We had crab cakes and Waldorf salads, and he told me about the old days in the meatpacking industry, up until the closure of Union Stockyard in 1970.

I'd received instructions from both Shell and Herb prior to the date. From Shell, I was told to be polite, attentive, and complimentary. I was to ask questions, laugh at jokes, and seem interested without getting too personal. From Herb, I was told to check in with him every five minutes by using the code word *fascinating*, which signaled him to respond in my earpiece. If something was going wrong, I was to use the word *disaster*, which meant he'd come running. Also, if Mr. Sarcotti got too frisky, Herb advised me to go for the balls.

After lunch, and a polite kiss on the cheek from Mr. Sarcotti (no ball-kicking necessary), I was debriefed by Shell, who informed me that Mr. Sarcotti had spoken to him and I was his new favorite, and that the fee Mr. Sarcotti and others were paying to take me out was going toward my Armani outfit. Then I got ready for my theater and dinner date with Jeroen ten Berge.

A few minutes before my scheduled pick-up time—Shell had insisted all clients pick up their dates at the agency rather than meet them elsewhere because of the recent murders— there was a knock on my apartment door. My new apartment, by the way, was fabulous. Tidy, luxurious, well-furnished, and it came with maid service. It sure beat the hell out of dressing up like a hooker and arresting perverts.

I checked the peephole, saw it was Herb, and let him in.

Herb whistled when he walked in. "Nice threads."

I was wearing a little black cocktail dress that Amy Peterson, one of Shell's escorts, had lent me. "It's a Versace," I said. "Is that good?"

"It looks good."

"Shell bought it for her. He apparently buys clothes for all of his escorts."

Herb raised an eyebrow. "What do you think of that?"

"What I think is that I've never met a group of this many suspects outside of an Agatha Christie book. Seriously, Herb. Every one of them is nuts. Gloria thinks she's Marilyn Monroe. Sandy's already killed someone. Mizz Lizzy popped out of *Grimm's Fairy Tales* and looks like she's searching for children to cook and eat. Amy has her closet arranged so it's color-coded like a Roy G. Biv rainbow—"

"Roy G. Biv?"

I shook my head, laughing. "You know…red, orange, yellow, green, blue, indigo, violet."

"Where does black fit in?"

"Black, white, and shades of gray have to go into another closet."

"What about prints? Or plaid?"

"I didn't ask. She started talking about astrological signs and palm reading, so I faked a headache and got out of there. Is it possible a woman is the murderer?"

"We can't rule it out. I've never heard of any female serial killers, but I agree the ladies here are a bit…odd. Shell vouches for this Jeroen guy, says he's a harmless old man, but I'll be tagging along just the same. Can you help me with your mic?"

Half an hour later, a limo picked me up at the agency. Jeroen ten Berge was a distinguished older gentleman, silver haired, well-dressed, quick to share the champagne he had chilling. I restricted myself to one glass, then played Miss Attentive through the car ride to Ninety-fifth and Kedzie, and on into dinner at the Martinique, the restaurant attached to the Drury Lane Theater.

Jeroen—pronounced *yer-oh-in*—was a delightful man. A retired investment banker who still dabbled in the stock market, he was a treasure trove of stories and jokes, and the perfect dining companion. Halfway into our chicken vesuvio, he asked me the same thing Mr. Sarcotti had asked.

"How can a vivacious, delightful woman such as yourself still be single?"

I played coy. "I could ask you the same thing, Jeroen. An interesting man like you could probably take your pick of grateful brides. Why aren't you married?"

His face sank. "I was, for thirty-eight wonderful years. My wife passed in '86. Breast cancer."

I regretted the question. Especially since Shell warned me not to get too personal.

"I'm sorry."

"I'm not. Maria was the best thing that ever happened to me. My best friend. My lover. My soul mate. I was so lucky to have so many good years with her, even if the last few were hard." He leaned closer, put his hand on mine. "Life isn't worth living unless you have someone to share it with, Jacqueline. The good times, and the bad times. In sickness and in health. Even toward the end, she could still make my heart flutter when I looked at her."

"She sounds lovely," I said, meaning it.

"I'm a rich, successful man, Jacqueline. But I would trade it all—the money, the houses, the entire stock portfolio—for just one more day with Maria. Success means nothing unless you have someone to share it with."

Jeroen's eyes glassed over. I gave his hand a squeeze, and we finished our meal in silence. I excused myself to go to the bathroom, and checked in with Herb.

"I made my date cry," I said into my bra-concealed microphone.

"Remember you're a cop, not an escort," Herb said in my ear piece. He hadn't been able to secure tickets to the show, or afford the restaurant, so he was in the parking lot eating a sandwich his wife had packed for him. *"Besides, it sounds like he was a very lucky guy to have a woman he cared so much for."*

"Would you do that, Herb? Give up your career for your wife?"

"I'd give up anything for my wife."

After dinner, we watched the musical comedy *They're Playing Our Song*. Jeroen had seen it in New York, and cheerily mouthed the song lyrics along with the performers. By the end of the play he was no longer maudlin, and during the limo ride back, he convinced me to have another glass of champagne. When he dropped me off and said goodnight, I got a chaste kiss on the cheek.

I was left wanting more. Not from Jeroen. From life. I wanted someone who would give up everything for me.

But would I be willing to do the same for someone else?

For Alan?

Present day

2010, August 10

00:15:03...00:15:02...00:15:01...

Fifteen minutes to live.

As I watched the clock, I was oddly philosophical. Once I realized death was inevitable, a cold sort of calm came over me. I was sure there would be fear and panic later, but for the moment, I was retaining some objectivity.

I kind of felt like I was still in college, waiting to get the results of a test. I'd lived for forty-nine years. I'd done things, both good and not so good. I'd tried my best, worked my ass off, pursued and reached my goals.

Now I wanted my final grade.

Did I lead an A+ life?

An A?

At least a B+?

I'd taken some very bad people off the streets. I'd helped a lot of innocent folks. I'd saved some lives. I was a pretty good cop.

On a more personal level, I had loved and been loved. Made friends. Had some fun. Saw some interesting things. Learned a lot.

Was that enough for a B?

My marriage had failed. I'd lost people close to me. Made some big mistakes. Had some big regrets.

Does that get me at least a B-?

Of all my regrets, the one that hurt the most, especially now, was never having children. I'd always been so busy. So dedicated to my job. So intent on saving the world. It would have been nice to have a kid, to pass on some of this wisdom I'd learned, to...

Oh shit.

The memory came stampeding back, making me catch my breath. The memory of last night, clear and focused and full-blown. Standing in the bedroom, looking at Phin in bed, drowsy from his chemotherapy and medication, wanting so badly to tell him about the pregnancy test I just took.

The positive pregnancy test.

I was going to be a mother.

Phin was going to be a father.

I hadn't expected to see the double line on the little test stick. In truth, I thought the reason for my missed period was the onset of menopause.

But it wasn't menopause. It was a baby.

A tiny human being, growing inside me.

A miniature version of me. A child. A legacy.

A miracle.

The weight of this realization came crashing down on me, hard. With thirteen minutes left on the countdown clock, I quit being melancholy and reflective, and began to saw the rope with renewed vigor, ignoring the pain in my tortured wrists.

I had to get out of there. For the two of us.

Three years ago
2007, August 8

A few seconds after we pulled into the Dominick's parking lot, the Special Response Team showed up. The FedEx guy, a scruffy redhead named Gordy, had placed Dalton's package in an empty parking spot, then stood a safe distance away, alongside me and Herb, to watch the bomb squad have at it.

"I hope it's not a big box of anthrax," Gordy said. "I sniffed that sucker. Sniffed it good. Do you think it could be anthrax?"

"No."

"Smallpox?"

"No."

"Botulism? We just had a botulism epidemic in the city."

"It's not botulism," I said, pretty sure of myself.

"Ebola?"

I gave the guy a WTF look. "Ebola?"

"I saw it on the Science Channel. You start bleeding blood from your pores. Then your skin comes off. I hope it isn't Ebola."

I hoped it wasn't Ebola, too. But I didn't think it was any sort of disease. Or explosive. Mr. K didn't operate like that. He was hands-on.

The SRT, in full bomb suits, performed a battery of tests on the box, using various pieces of expensive-looking equipment. I recognized a portable X-ray unit and a boroscope—a flexible camera usually used by doctors giving rectal exams. After ten minutes of poking and prodding, the SRT sergeant tugged off his helmet and chest plate and approached us.

"Is it Ebola?" Gordy asked.

"It's a bottle, Lieutenant." He gave Gordy a sideways glance and then handed me the boroscope, showing me the color screen. "Looks like the seal is intact."

I instantly recognized the familiar shape. I'd seen it many times before. "Thanks for your help, Sergeant. I think I can take it from here."

"Do you want us to open it?"

"I think I can handle it."

I approached the box, feeling no fear, pretty sure of what this package was. Dalton wouldn't have sent me anything incriminating, because there was the possibility I would have gotten it before he left the country, and subsequently arrested him.

No, he didn't send this to threaten me or harm me physically. This had a different purpose.

"What is it, Jack?" Herb was walking alongside me.

"Mr. K has two signatures. One is ball gags. What's the other?"

"Rubbing salt in his victims' wounds."

"That's what this is," I said, tearing off the box top.

As expected, there was a full bottle of Jack Daniels Tennessee Whiskey. Dalton's way of telling me he had won. And rubbing it in. There was also a handwritten note:

By now, I'm on my way to Cape Verde, and there's nothing you can do about it. I'll likely never set foot in the U.S. again. I want you to know that I gave you a fair chance to catch me. The clues were there. You simply weren't good enough. Don't be too hard on yourself. You can't win them all.

I knew I couldn't win them all. It went with the Job.

But I really *really* wanted to win this one.

Twenty-one years ago
1989, August 17

"*Want to take a little walk?*" Herb asked in my ear.
I'd just stepped out of Jeroen's limo and was staring at Shell's building, about to go inside.

"Where to?" I said into my bra microphone.

"*Around the block. Like you've decided to have a drink after dinner. Find a spot and park yourself at the bar.*"

"Where are you?"

"*Across the street.*"

I resisted the urge to look for him, and instead headed east down Ohio, toward Michigan Avenue. It was close to midnight, but there were still a few folks wandering the streets. Not as many as if it were a weekend, but enough that snatching me would be risky.

Then again, the killer had snatched three other women without drawing any attention.

It was dark, hot, and humid. The city smelled like garbage. A car cruised up, slowing down as it neared me. I wobbled a little, swaying left and right, forcing myself to giggle.

"How much did you have to drink?" Herb asked.

"Just a glass of wine. I'm playing the part, making myself an easy target. You see this car?"

The car was a Cadillac. Black. The windows were slightly tinted, so I couldn't see inside. It pulled into the alley ahead of me. I stopped, forcing myself not to reach for the gun in my purse, feeling my arteries throb with adrenaline as the passenger-side window lowered.

"Need a ride, pretty lady?"

"Shell," I said, blowing out the breath I'd been holding.

He was wearing yet another tailored suit, this one tan corduroy with patches on the elbows, and his hair was slicked back with gel. "What are you doing out here, all by yourself?"

"My job," I said.

He winced. "Sorry. Forgot you were a cop for a second there. Saw one of my girls walking by herself and my overly protective nature kicked in. Will you be trolling killers for a while? Or are you free for a drink?"

"This guy is starting to bug me," Herb said.

"Yeah," I replied.

"Great," said Shell, who thought I was talking to him. "Hop in."

Oops. "How about we grab something nearby?" I wanted to stay in the area. All three women had disappeared within a few blocks of the agency.

"There's this classy bar on Wabash. Miller's Pub."

"Miller's Pub?" I repeated, for Herb's benefit.

"I know it," Herb said. *"I can meet you there."*

"You're on," I said, to both Herb and Shell.

I walked around the car, climbing into the passenger seat. Shell smelled like cologne. Somehow, that made me think of Alan, who never wore cologne. I hadn't called Alan all day. Partly because I'd been busy. Partly because I still wasn't sure what to say to him.

"You know what I feel like?" Shell drummed his fingers on the steering wheel as he pulled onto the street. "Dancing. Want to go dancing?"

"I'm not really in a dancing mood, Shell."

"Do you like music?"

"Sure."

"How about Buddy Guy's?"

Buddy Guy was a Chicago blues legend. He owned a club on Wabash, not too far from Miller's.

"Buddy Guy's," I said. Herb didn't respond. I wondered if he was out of radio range.

"I saw Clapton play there once. Just came in, unannounced, jammed with Buddy's band. Amazing show."

"Okay," I said, raising my voice to near yelling, "let's go to Buddy Guy's Legends. Buddy Guy's Legends, on Wabash."

Shell gave me a look like I'd grown an extra head. Still no reply from Herb. I could only hope he'd heard.

A few minutes later, Shell was pulling into a multilevel parking garage on Balbo, where he found a spot on the third floor. We took the brightly lit stairwell down to street level, and walked a block to the bar.

There was a small line. We queued up behind a couple of blue-collar black guys.

A lonely-looking fat man got in line behind us. Shell paid my five-dollar cover, and once inside we took everything in, looking for a place to sit.

Everything about Buddy Guy's screamed *the blues*. The dim lighting, the smell of cigarette smoke and whiskey, the plaintive whine of a single electric guitar, the bartender building drinks and sticking them on damp, empty trays, the sad-faced patrons, many of them sitting alone, nursing something strong. Shell and I found a corner table, so dark I had to lean close to see him. A waitress—who looked like she'd gone three hard rounds with disappointment before it knocked her down for the count—stood next to us without uttering a word, her order pad in hand. Shell got a martini. I got red wine, then excused myself to go to the ladies' room, having to shout to be heard over the amplifier feedback.

It was quieter in there, but not by much. I fussed with my mic and earpiece, trying to reach Herb, but didn't get any indication he heard me. Either he was still looking for parking, or he'd gone to Miller's. The smart thing to do was have a quick drink, then head back to the agency. I really didn't think Shell was the killer, especially since he was the one who sought out police help. Besides, I had my Beretta in my purse.

I met Shell back at our table. Our drinks still hadn't come. I spotted them, sitting lonely on the bar, our waitress nowhere to be seen. Shell bent close and said something, but I couldn't hear anything because we were too close to the speakers. The drinks eventually came. The gravelly-voiced singer bemoaned his cheating woman, his lost job, his dead dog, and his worsening bursitis. I just closed my eyes and let the music take me where it wanted. The wine was cheap and bitter. After two sips, I didn't want any more.

Shell slammed his martini, smiled, and then pointed at my glass with a raised eyebrow. I shook my head. He raised his hand to signal our waitress, and I leaned over to stop him, to tell him I was tired and wanted to go.

As I leaned forward, the whole bar seemed to rock, like we were on a boat during a storm. I felt as if I was falling. I reached out, trying to stop the world from moving, knocking over my wine glass. My head hit Shell's shoulder, and he grinned at me, and as he grinned his face got darker and darker until all I saw was a rolling, swirling blackness that swallowed me up.

Present day
2010, August 10

"Got a match," Herb said, hanging up the phone. "The prints, and McGlade's picture, belong to a man named Luther Kite."

They were still five minutes from the prison, even with Phin blowing through red lights and stop signs and crushing the accelerator.

"Why does that name sound familiar?" Harry asked.

"Remember the Kinnakeet Ferry Massacre? It made the national headlines seven years ago. Involved that horror author, Andrew Z. Thomas, who went nuts and started killing people back in the nineties. Kite has an outstanding warrant for his connection to the murders, and he's the prime suspect for a killing spree across North Carolina right before the ferry slaughter. Hung a woman off a lighthouse."

"Record?" Phin asked, eyes stuck to the road.

"Not much. Arrested for animal cruelty. Resulted in a fine. Seems he skinned some cats."

Phin waited for Harry to say something flippant, but McGlade remained eerily silent.

"Kite and Thomas have been on the lam for seven years," Herb continued. "We know there were two people watching the house, and gassing you and Jack while you sleep sounds like something a writer would dream up. Now that we've got a solid connection, we should get the media involved."

Phin nodded. Herb got on the phone again, began making calls. By the time he was finished, everyone in Chicago, Illinois, Indiana, and Wisconsin would be looking for Jack, Andrew Z. Thomas, and Luther Kite.

Phin hoped it would be enough.

Three years ago
2007, August 8

Herb and I sat in my car, parked outside Dalton's building. It was going on ten p.m., and he hadn't come home yet. A team followed him from Spill to Bradstreet's palatial estate in the neighboring suburb of Evanston.

"I tell you," Herb said, "that bottle of Jack Daniels is looking better and better."

I agreed. I could use a drink. Herb and I were both tired, depressed, and discouraged. Nothing was panning out. The boy hadn't matched any recent missing person reports, and hadn't been identified yet. We'd even given the picture to the TV stations to air, but so far, no hits.

Tom and a rotating crew of ten cops were continuing to call storage facilities within a thirty-mile radius, asking about locker 515, with not a single promising lead. Hajek, from the crime lab, had done a full workup of the photo, and the only thing he could tell us was it appeared to have been altered somehow. Hajek believed the color and contrast had been enhanced. He had passed it on to a colleague who knew more

177

about photographic manipulation, and we were waiting to hear back.

Still no ID on the John Doe who died on the Catherine Wheel. And after calling four different judges and pleading our case, none would sign an arrest warrant for Dalton or a search warrant for his condo.

Things weren't looking good for our heroes. Which is why I brightened up when Herb said, "Let's break in."

"You serious?" I asked.

"He's probably playing it safe, spending the night at the lawyer's. Maybe we'll find something in his home."

"Wouldn't stand up," I said. Any evidence we found would be inadmissible in court.

"I care about the kid, not a conviction. Besides, the wallet gave me an idea. What if his passport is in his house?"

I nodded, getting it. If we swiped Dalton's passport, he wouldn't be able to leave the country. Those things took weeks to renew. That would give us more time to hang something on him.

"First we break into his car, then we try to frame him, then we steal his wallet, now we're going to burgle his residence. Not our finest day, Herb."

"While we're inside, I may also piss on his sofa."

I had a gym bag in the trunk. I took out my sweats and put the cement-filled milk jug and some yellow tape inside. Then walked across the street to 1300 North Lake Shore. It was a new doorman, and we flashed our badges and took the elevator to Dalton's condo. As far as disciplinary action went, I doubted we'd get into any trouble for this little action. Dalton wouldn't be able to press charges from Cape Verde. That is, if he even knew we were the ones who broke in.

We stood outside his door, and I gave it a gentle knock. When no one answered, I asked Herb, "Did you hear a scream coming from inside, prompting us to enter without a warrant?"

"I heard a scream, and also smelled smoke," Herb said. "It's our duty as police officers to break in and try to save lives. Plus, the door was already broken when we got here."

I hefted the milk jug. "Did you notice a burglar alarm when we were here earlier?"

"Nope."

"Me neither."

I reared back and swung the makeshift battering ram with everything I had, just to the right of the doorknob. There was a loud *CRACK* and the door burst inward, the jamb throwing splinters. I went in low and fast, drawing my Colt from my shoulder holster, quickly scanning the hallway. Then I made my way through the rest of the condo, Herb at my heels. When we deemed it empty, Herb got started putting some yellow CRIME SCENE tape over the doorway. If anyone walked by and noticed the door, the tape would prevent them from calling the cops, because the cops obviously already knew about it.

Though Dalton's condo was massive—far bigger than my house in Bensenville—it was pretty easy to search because there wasn't anything there. Even though it was fully furnished, there were no personal items of any kind, other than books. No letters, or bills, or photo albums. No computer. No clothing. No passport.

"Fridge is empty," Herb said.

I went back to the hallway, staring at the pictures on the walls. Dalton had said he'd taken those photos. I didn't have much of an artistic eye, but they seemed a bit drab and lifeless to me. Even the shot of his house on the beach made a tropical paradise seem rather bland.

There were six pictures total, three on each side. Besides the house, there was a shot of an empty cornfield, a shot of the Chicago skyline, one of some trees in the winter, and one of a sunset over a lake. The only one with a human figure was of a house, with a woman sitting on the porch. The picture was taken far enough away that the woman's features were tough to make out, beyond the fact that she had long, dark hair and was Caucasian. She could have been anywhere from eighteen to fifty, and the clothing she wore—a blouse and shorts—didn't lend itself to being dated.

On a hunch, I took the picture from the wall and then spent a minute removing it from the frame. The back of the photo had something written on it.

5CHAUMBURG 1995

"What do you think?" I asked Herb, who was peering over my shoulder.

"No idea. Maybe it's one of his victims?"

"If Dalton is Mr. K, he's too careful for that. He wouldn't ever let anything lead back to him."

"A girlfriend? Relative?"

"Not a very personal photo. Normally, if you take a picture of someone you care about, don't you move in for a closer shot?"

Herb shrugged. "Maybe the woman doesn't matter. He's got the whole house in the frame. Maybe the house is what's important. Or maybe it doesn't mean anything, and is no more personal than the cornfield or the sunset."

I frowned. My subconscious was nagging at me, trying to tell me something, but I couldn't get it to come forward. While I was thinking, I began to liberate the other photos from their frames. Herb joined in. We didn't discover any more writing, or anything else that would have been useful, like a signed confession, or a map showing where bodies were buried.

My cell rang. I slapped it to my face.

"Daniels."

"Lieut, it's Tom Mankowski. We may have a hit on the storage locker."

"What did you find, Tom?"

"National Storage. They've got a unit rented out to John Smith. Unit 515."

Smith was the name Dalton had used for his victim at the U-Store-It on Fullerton.

"We'll meet you there," I said.

Then Herb and I hurried for the elevator.

Present day
2010, August 10

I had no idea how long the digital countdown clock had been blinking 00:00:00. It may have only been for a few seconds. It may have been several minutes. I was so totally absorbed in trying to get free that I'd blocked out all other fears, thoughts, and senses.

So it was quite a shock when I saw Mr. K standing there, staring down at me.

"Hello, Jack. It's been a while."

My wrists—bleeding profusely now—still weren't free.

I didn't make it. I was too late.

Then Mr. K pulled something out of his pocket. Small and white, and possibly the most horrifying thing I'd ever been shown.

My pregnancy test.

"Isn't this delightful," he said. "Now I get to kill two for the price of one."

Twenty-one years ago
1989, August 17

I woke up groggy, disoriented, nauseous.

I didn't know where I was, didn't remember how I got there. The floor beneath me was cold, concrete, suggesting a basement or garage. It was too dark to see anything. My hands fluttered around me, trying to judge the size of the area, and I realized with a start that I was completely naked.

This was bad. Real bad.

What the hell happened to me?

I filled my lungs, ready to shout for help, and then stopped myself right before any sound came out.

Maybe it wasn't a good idea to let whoever had me know I was awake.

Though I'd been in some hairy situations during my rookie years, I couldn't say any of them was life and death. Once, my partner Harry and I had been shot at, but the perp had been so far away there had been no real danger. Another time, a suspect took a swing at me when I asked to see some ID. I'd slipped the blow, and what followed was the only time

I'd ever used my police baton, hitting him in the knee hard enough to break it.

But neither of those were as nerve-jangling as waking up naked in some unknown basement.

I listened, hearing some machine hum in the background. Sniffing the air, I detected something foul. Beneath the mildew and dampness there was a cloying, rotten meat smell that reminded me of the morgue.

Thinking of the morgue made me remember the last time I was there, with Harry and Herb and Shell.

Shell.

It came back in snatches, like short movie clips. Sitting in a theater, watching Jeroen sing along with the show. Driving in the limousine. Walking down the street and getting into Shell's car. Listening to blues.

Did I drink too much? Pass out?

My head felt big, stuffy. Not a hangover feeling. More like when I was young and had a bad cold and Mom kept spooning cough medicine into me.

Drugged. I'd been drugged.

I got on all fours, began to crawl in the direction I was facing, moving slowly and reaching out ahead of me so I didn't bump into anything. My arms and legs felt heavy, and they didn't respond well to my mental commands. After traversing a few feet, I came to a wall. Concrete again, confirming my suspicion this was a basement.

Bracing myself against the wall, I managed to get onto my feet. My head didn't want to stay upright on my neck, and my eyes didn't want to stay open. I forced myself to hyperventilate, thinking the influx of oxygen might help make the drug wear off faster. Once I was confident I wouldn't topple over, I began to follow the wall to my right, toward the machine sound. I was cautious, afraid of hitting my head or tripping over something. My fears were unwarranted; the basement seemed to be completely empty.

I reached a corner, getting my fingers snared in the world's largest spider web, rubbing my palms together to get it off while trying not to imagine black widows jumping into my hair. Adjusting my direction, following the new wall, I closed in on the mechanical hum.

The sound was familiar. I was pretty sure I knew what it was.

A few steps later, I touched it. Big. Square. Vibrating slightly beneath my palms.

A refrigerator.

Actually, two refrigerators, side by side.

This was good. Fridges had lights. If I opened the doors, I'd be able to see.

I sought the handle of the closer one, stepped back, and pulled.

No light came on. And the rancid meat smell got worse.

Reaching a tentative hand inside, fearful I'd touch something awful, I began to explore the fridge.

It was empty. Even the drawers and the racks were gone. I thought back to the morgue, to Phil Blasky and his assertion that the body had been kept in a refrigerator.

Shivering, I reached for its companion.

I really didn't want to open it. But at the same time, I knew I had to.

Filling my lungs, blowing out a deep breath, I stood in front of the second fridge.

Just do it.

I yanked the door open, staring inside.

Ten sets of eyes stared back at me, belonging to the ten human heads stacked neatly on the refrigerator's wire shelves.

Present day
2010, August 10

When Phin saw Jack on the iPhone screen, tied up on the floor and helpless, he wanted to put his fist through the wall.

"There are, ah, controls," Warden Miller said. He was a meaty, red-faced man who had a mustache that rivaled Herb's. "If you tap the image, you can zoom in, move the camera a bit."

Grinding his molars, Phin followed Miller's instructions and a white cross appeared on the screen, superimposed over Jack. By touching different parts, he could pan and tilt. Two white dots, when pressed, let him move in and out. Phin got a close-up of Jack's terrified, crying face, a ball gag in her mouth. Then the man in the room with her stood in front of the camera, blocking the shot. The man wore a hat, the overhead camera view making it impossible to see his face.

"You talked to Brotsky?" Phin asked the warden. He felt as if his veins were full of antifreeze.

"He's not saying anything."

"Can we talk to him?" Herb asked. He was standing over Phin's shoulder. Harry sat in the chair across the warden's expansive desk, with his face in his hands.

"Of course," Miller said. "We've got him in the isolation unit."

Driving into the visitor's parking lot of Stateville Correctional Center made Phin feel a bit nervous. After all, he was wanted for several crimes, and Stateville might be where he wound up if he were ever caught. The complex itself seemed to be designed for the express purpose of intimidating anyone who walked in. A thirty-foot-high concrete wall, topped with razor wire, surrounded the institution. The main buildings were called *round houses*, and as their name implied, they were circular, with the cells arranged along the walls. In the center of each was a watchtower. This design was known as *panopticon*, which made the inmates feel that at any given time, they were being watched by the guards.

Warden Miller led the trio down an officious-looking hallway, through a barred security door, and into a very long corridor. The air was warm, stuffy, and smelled like sweat and desperation. Phin clenched the iPhone in his hand, watching the image. He wished there was audio, because the man seemed to be talking. Then he lifted his head up and stared right into the camera. Phin didn't recognize the guy—he didn't have long black hair like Luther Kite supposedly did. But Kite easily could have cut and dyed it.

"Herb, Harry, check out this man's face."

They crowded in around him, but as soon as they did, the man's face was obscured by something he was holding up to the camera. Something small and thin, made of white plastic.

Phin zoomed out, trying to focus, and the lens adjusted automatically—

—showing two clear blue lines on Jack's pregnancy test. The one Phin hadn't been able to find.

"Is that...?" Harry's voice trailed off.

"Jesus Christ." Herb put his hand over his mouth. "She's pregnant."

Phin felt the edges of his vision get dark. He quickly handed off the phone to Harry and then turned away, dropping to his knees, clutching his belly as he threw up on the tile floor.

Three years ago
2007, August 8

Six Corners used to be an historic shopping district, clustered around an intersection where Milwaukee Avenue, Cicero Avenue, and Irving Park Road all intersected.

National Storage was housed in a six-level brownstone, and Tom Mankowski, along with his partner, Roy Lewis, were standing on the sidewalk in front. Tom was tall, lean, and in profile he looked a lot like the image of Thomas Jefferson on the nickel. Roy was a bit stockier, broader in the shoulders, and resembled the boxer Marvin Hagler.

I parked in front of a fire hydrant, figuring I'd disregarded the law so many times that day, once more wouldn't matter. I normally wasn't such an *ends justifies the means* type of person, but endanger the life of a child and I was willing to be flexible.

"Have you been inside yet?" I asked as we approached. Both men wore suits, as befitting Homicide detectives, though Roy's fit better and was less rumpled.

"Just got here, when we saw your bucket roll up," Roy said.

"My bucket?" I said.

Roy became sheepish. "I meant your classic vintage automobile, Lieutenant."

I turned to Tom. "Background on John Smith?"

"Manager wouldn't reveal personal details over the phone. Said we had to show up in person and prove we were cops before he gave us an address."

"Then let's go prove it."

The lobby was a step up from Merle's U-Store-It, and contained a water cooler and several floor plants, along with a security camera hanging on the wall. The watchman sat behind a large desk, sans bulletproof glass. His nametag read AL. He was in his sixties, and had a gray pompadour that rivaled the King's during his *Blue Hawaii* years. He also smelled like he took a bath in cheap cigars.

"You the cops?" Al asked.

All four of us flashed our tin.

Al nodded. "I took the liberty of pulling up John Smith's rental agreement."

He tapped some papers on his desk, which Herb snatched up. It was refreshing to deal with someone cooperative for a change.

"Do you recall what John Smith looks like?" I asked.

"No idea. We got close to a thousand units here, and six other employees." He reached into his desk and pulled out half a cigar.

"Can we check out his locker?"

He nodded. "Absolutely. We reserve the right to examine the contents of our renters' units if we believe they contain dangerous or illegal materials."Al jammed the cigar into the hinge of his mouth, then pulled a bolt cutter from under his desk. "Let's go and see."

We walked down an access hall, to the freight elevator.

"According to this, John Smith lives in Portage Park," Herb said, reading the paperwork. "Paid by credit card. He's had the unit for two months."

I wasn't feeling good about this one. John Smith was a common name, and it was doubtful Dalton would rent a locker somewhere with security cameras.

"What's this guy done?" the manager asked just as the lift arrived. "Kill somebody? Drugs? Kill somebody for drugs?"

"We think he's smuggling Cuban cigars," Tom said. "You ever have a Cuban?"

"Years ago. Best thing I ever put in my mouth."

"These are special cigars," Tom said, "full leaf wrappers, rolled between the thighs of promiscuous women."

Apparently Tom didn't feel good about this one either.

The elevator spit us out on the fifth floor, and Al led us to unit 515. Wielding the bolt cutters with apparent enthusiasm, Al snapped off the combination lock and gripped the door handle. He pulled it up in a quick, smooth motion, lifting the door up on rollers, and we all got one of the biggest surprises of our lives.

Twenty-one years ago
1989, August 17

The severed heads were all female, lined up carefully on the refrigerator shelves so they all stared at me. Some were more decomposed than others, the bluing flesh decaying and clinging to the bone, making them appear mummified. Others were so fresh they almost looked ready to start speaking.

Each of their faces was grotesquely slathered with makeup. Fire-engine red lipstick, thickly applied and wider than the actual mouth. Pink rouge bright on the pale cheeks. Their wide eyes—their most shocking feature—were missing eyelids, the sockets framed in dark eyeliner. Some of the eyes were milky white. Others had begun to shrivel, like raisins.

The stench blasted over me, prompting a gag. I slammed the fridge closed and backed up, once again plunging the basement into darkness. Every square inch of my naked body had broken out in goosebumps. I stood there for a moment, my mind wrestling with the horror I'd just seen, the implications of it. I tried to swallow, but my throat was too tight. This was so far removed from anything I considered reality, I felt a mental break, a disconnect. Like I was watching someone else go through this, instead of experiencing it myself.

I blew out a big breath, so hard my cheeks puffed out. Awful as it was, I knew what I needed to do.

I had to escape, and get help.

In order to do that, I needed light.

Reaching out through the darkness, I groped for the refrigerator door handle. My fingers locked around it, and I questioned my will to actually open it again, to view the obscenity once more.

I pulled.

The heads stared back, their dead eyes boring into me.

Leaving the door open, I turned around, taking in my surroundings, needing to concentrate. The overhead metal girders and steel support beams confirmed that I was in a basement. A small basement, with two windows sealed with glass blocks. There was a wooden staircase in the near corner, leading up to a closed door. A water heater and furnace stood against the far wall.

I needed a weapon, but nothing jumped out at me. Wincing, I once again focused on the refrigerator. The freezer door was still closed. Much as I didn't want to, perhaps there was something in there that could help me. I crept up to it, braced myself, and tugged the door open.

Empty.

Then, from upstairs, I head a soul-shattering, mind-blowing scream.

Present day
2010, August 10

M r. K stares down at Jack Daniels, her teary eyes wide with fear.

She is indeed something special. It's almost a shame to reduce her to the squealing, pleading animal she would soon become.

He has killed a hundred and sixty-three people. He's sure of this number, because he took meticulous notes. They always end the same way, terrified and screaming, bleeding and gasping. Even the strong ones, the hard ones, the brave ones, eventually broke.

Broke is the correct word for it. When enough pain is induced, human beings cease to be human anymore. They revert to a primal state, with no higher reasoning.

This will quite possibly be the last murder of his illustrious career, and he almost didn't take this job. But it seemed like a fitting, final chapter to his life. A satisfying last act, to neatly bookend all that came before.

Plus, the money was extraordinary.

"Victor Brotsky sends his regards, Lieutenant," he says, pointing up at the overhead camera. "He paid me a great deal to be here for this historic event. I find it fitting that he chose me, don't you?"

Jack screams something into her gag.

"You'll get a chance to talk soon," Mr. K says. "I'm going to put you under for a moment. When you wake up, you'll be on the Catherine Wheel. Then we'll begin. I must say, I was quite surprised to find that pregnancy test in your bathroom garbage. You didn't think this is a bit of a late start? Why did you wait so long to have a baby, Jack? Had you done so at a reasonable age, your child could be in college by now. Instead, its life will be over before it has even begun."

Mr. K opens up the black bag he's brought along, taking out a syringe and a glass vial.

"Luckily, I still have some friends in town. Medical supplies are so hard to get on short notice."

He sticks the needle in the vial, filling it with the sedative, plunging it into Jack's arm. As her eyelids begin to flutter, Mr. K takes another item out of the bag, holding it in front of Jack's face.

"Take this, for example. You can't simply waltz into any drugstore and buy a high-grade speculum like this one."

Jack screams once more as she drifts away to unconsciousness.

Three years ago
2007, August 8

"That's just...*wrong*," Tom said.

The five of us were gaping at the contents of John Smith's storage unit. The twenty-by-twenty-foot locker was populated by lawn gnomes. Hundreds of them. They were all lined up in rows, each maybe eighteen inches tall. Red, pointy hats. Green suits. White beards.

"There's a whole army of them," Tom said. "Like they're ready to march out of here and fight a tiny little war."

"That settles it." Herb nodded his head, his chins jiggling. "I'm buying a lottery ticket later."

"Buy one for me, too," I told him.

As far as lawn gnomes went, these weren't particularly attractive. Their pinched, elvin faces had odd, shocked expressions on them, and their backs were bowed, as if suffering from some sort of gnome scoliosis.

"What is wrong with you white people?" Roy asked.

"Excuse me?" Al said.

"You don't see no brothers putting these creepy little fuckers out on their lawns."

"How about that one?" Herb asked, pointing.

One of the gnomes had brown skin.

"I am not seeing that," Roy said, shaking his head. "That doesn't exist for me."

I tilted slightly left, then right. The gnomes seemed to be tracking my movement, their eyes following me. It was eerie.

"Maybe they're filled with cocaine," Tim said, bending over and picking one up.

They weren't filled with cocaine. They were just what they seemed to be—hideous decorator items for the lawn and garden. Al closed up the door and snapped on a new padlock.

"Someone owes me seven fifty for the replacement lock," he muttered. "Cuban cigars my ass."

Twenty minutes later, we were all headed back to the station. There were over three hundred more storage facilities to call, and we had less than ten hours before Dalton's digital watch reached zero.

Twenty-one years ago
1989, August 17

The scream came from directly above me. A high-pitched shrill cry of pure agony. It went on for over a minute, pausing only long enough for quick gulps of breath.

Then, abruptly, it stopped.

My mind betrayed me, casting images of torture and pain so extreme I was paralyzed with inaction. I kept seeing that slideshow from the police academy, of the atrocities committed upon that woman at the hands of Mr. K.

Could that be Mr. K above me? Plying his skills upon some poor victim?

Maybe the only reason the screaming stopped was because his victim was now gagged.

Or maybe the victim had died. Which meant he'd be coming for me next.

I thought about Shell. Could he be a part of this somehow? He'd had the opportunity to drug my drink.

I thought about Herb. Could he have known we'd gone to Buddy Guy's? Was there a chance he was outside right now, about to come storming in?

Or maybe Herb had already stormed in. That scream could have been male.

Forcing myself to move, I went to the nearest window. The glass blocks were thick—no way I'd break them with anything less than a hammer. Creeping to the stairs, giving the refrigerator a wide berth, I knelt down and pried at the bottom wooden step, trying to lift it. No good; it was on too tight.

Peering up at the door at the top of the flight, I wondered if there was any chance at all it might be open. Whatever drug I'd been given was strong. It knocked me out in just two sips. But perhaps my abductor was used to his victims being unconscious for longer than I was, and there was no need to lock them in the basement.

Buoyed by the possibility, I slowly ascended the staircase. I felt each creak of the wood in my teeth. Every step was a battle between wanting to hurry, wanting to retreat, and forcing myself to go slow and steady to minimize the noise. By the time I reached the top of the flight, I was shivering, covered in cold sweat, my mouth so dry I couldn't swallow.

I put my ear to the door, listening.

Silence.

My shaking hand fit itself around the doorknob. Softly, carefully, I attempted to turn it—

—and the sucker actually turned.

It took the remaining bit of self-control I had left not to throw the door open and run like hell. I was naked, and had no idea where I was, or what time it was, or who had me. My best chance would be to find my gun, or a phone.

Setting my jaw, I eased the door open, praying for oiled hinges. It moved with minimal whining, and I stuck my sweaty head through the doorway and squinted down a dimly lit hall. The house was quiet. No movement. No human sounds. I stepped onto the tile floor, passing a crucifix hanging on the wall, passing a framed Nagel poster, passing a light switch that I desperately wanted to flip on.

The basement had been a hostile, foreign environment. But upstairs was an average, normal home. Horrible things shouldn't happen in a house like this, which made it even more frightening. Anyone walking into this modest dwelling couldn't possible guess that the basement had a refrigerator full of severed heads, or that the person who lived here liked to abduct and dismember women.

The hallway opened up into another room. I paused again, forcing myself to go slow, gingerly peering around the corner and seeing a living room.

There was a TV. A sofa. A floor lamp, the low-watt bulb under the shade glowing soft yellow. The window had curtains pulled shut, but I could see through the cracks it was night out. On a coffee table were several textbooks, including one that had *Social Studies: Teacher's Edition* written on the cover.

Then I heard something. A low, male voice, from someplace in the house. Too faint to make out any specific words.

I decided to run for it. Moving quickly, I found an adjacent hallway, located the front door, and gripped the knob.

It wouldn't budge. The door was solid, heavy wood, and the deadbolt was key activated.

Turning around, I went back into the living room, kneeling on the sofa, sweeping back the curtains.

The windows had bars over them, chained shut. I stared outside and saw I could have been in any number of Chicago neighborhoods. There were cars parked along both sides of the street. A sidewalk. Trees. My abductor had a neatly trimmed front lawn and a small flower garden with violets.

I got out of the living room, rounding another corner, stopping abruptly when I saw the phone hanging on the wall.

I picked it up, and the male voice I heard grew in volume tenfold, a foreign accent coming out of the receiver.

"—*take care of her soon. In fact, I'll do it right now. I just heard a click. I think she's awake and listening to us.*"

I let the phone fall, then turned and ran, rushing down the hall, finding the kitchen, skidding to a stop and then slipping on a slick, plastic tarp that had been set on the floor, my feet losing their grip, my ass hitting the ground, sliding forward into Shell.

He was lying on his back, clutching several coils of rope to his chest.

I was thinking to myself that I had to get out of there, that I didn't have time to untie him, and then I realized that it wasn't rope at all, it was his intestines, and I tried to crab-walk backwards but Shell's blood was all over me and I couldn't get any kind of traction, couldn't get away. His dead, open eyes were rolled back in his head, his mouth forever frozen with his final scream. Once he'd been a living, talking human being. I liked him. I'd kissed him. And now he was a cooling hunk of meat, profanely slaughtered, no trace left of the man I'd known.

Then someone walked in, filling the doorway. He was naked, thick, his hairy chest matted with blood. Slavic features, a dark, five o'clock shadow on his chubby face, which regarded me with amusement.

"My little cop girlfriend is awake," he said, his English tinged with a slight Russian accent. "My name is Victor Brotsky. We will have some fun, you and I. Yes?"

Then he raised up one of his meaty hands, and I noticed he was holding a butcher knife.

Present day
2010, August 10

Phin peered through the food tray slot in the door to the isolation cell. Victor Brotsky sat on his cot. He looked much older than his mug shot, which made sense—he'd been in prison for a long time. Brotsky was grayer, balder, and fatter than he was when first incarcerated. He wore dark blue slacks and a light blue shirt, the buttons straining against his barrel chest.

"You are wasting your time," he said. "I will tell you nothing."

Phin clenched his fists. He wanted to wrap his hands around Brotsky's fat neck and squeeze until he could feel the monster's heart stop beating.

Warden Miller called for two guards, dressed in riot gear, and they opened the cell door. Both had tasers at the ready. Brotsky didn't even bother to look over at them. His head was resting against the wall, eyes closed, his fingers tapping against his lap as if he was listening to music.

"Mr. Brotsky, I'm Sergeant Herb Benedict. I'm Lieutenant Daniels's partner."

Now Brotsky's eyes opened, focusing on the new arrivals. "Your partner, she is not looking so good lately."

"Where is my partner, Mr. Brotsky?"

"She is with an old friend of mine. Though perhaps *friend* is too strong a word, considering the amount of money he charged me."

"Your friend," Herb said, "is it Andrew Z. Thomas?"

"I do not know this person."

"Luther Kite?"

"I hired the best. He is an expert at what he does. Better, perhaps, than even me."

"I've got a deal for you," Harry said. He'd been quiet for so long, Phin had almost forgotten he'd come along. "I've got a hundred cartons of Marlboro Reds."

"I don't want your cigarettes, *svoloch*."

"They aren't for you," Harry said. "I'm giving a carton to every man who sticks a shiv in your ass in the shower. Two cartons if they fuck you after they stick you."

Brotsky smiled, and it was a chilling thing to witness. "I have been in here for more than a third of my life. You cannot scare me. You cannot hurt me. You cannot bribe me. The *sooka* cop will die in agony, and there is nothing you can do about it."

Phin turned to the warden. "I want ten minutes with him."

Miller looked pained. "I can't do that. I'm sorry."

"Just ten minutes. I promise I won't kill him."

"He's human garbage," Miller said. "I know that. But I can't willingly let an inmate be abused in my prison."

"The woman on the iPhone," Phin said. "She's pregnant with my child."

Brotsky barked out a wet laugh at this.

"Please," Phin said.

He took a step away from the warden, watching the guards in his peripheral vision. If Miller didn't go for it, Phin figured he could grab one of their tasers, lock himself inside the cell...

"Miller, let's talk for a second," Harry said. "In private."

Phin watched, helpless, as the two men walked down the corridor. Though it was torture to do so, Phin forced himself to look at the iPhone again. Jack was unconscious, and the man in the hat was pulling her across the floor, onto a large circle made of wood. There were straps for her arms and legs.

Phin also saw something small and shiny on the floor, next to Jack. He zoomed in.

It was a speculum.

Once again, Phin eyed the taser. If he hit the first guard in the throat, took his weapon, and fired it at the second guard, that would give him at least a minute alone with Brotsky. Longer if Harry and Herb guarded the door.

"I've decided to allow these gentlemen to settle their differences on their own," Warden Miller said. He was looking at his shoes. "You have ten minutes."

Phin shot Harry a glance. "Thanks."

"Make them count," Harry said. "And make this fat bastard feel every second."

Phin handed Herb the iPhone and stepped into the cell, hearing the steel door clang closed behind him.

"Now, we're going to have a little—"

Before Phin could finish, Victor Brotsky, all two hundred and seventy pounds of him, leapt up off the cot and slammed against Phin, knocking him to the floor.

Three years ago
2007, August 10

Dalton won.

We were up all night, calling twenty-four-hour storage facilities. When we ran out of those, Herb had the idea to call hotels, checking for guests in room 515.

We were still calling when Dalton's plane took off for Cape Verde.

In between calls, Herb, Tom, Roy, and I had devised several techniques to stall Dalton. Ramming into his car on the way to the airport. Calling TSA and saying he was a terrorist with a bomb. Arresting him on a made-up charge.

But we didn't attempt any of them. Much as I felt Dalton was Mr. K, I couldn't prove it. My duty, as a police officer, was to uphold and enforce the law. In the past two days, I'd failed at my duty. I not only failed to catch the bad guy, but I'd done a lot of things I wasn't proud of in my effort to catch him.

The end did not justify the means, because there was no end.

I said goodbye to Herb and was heading back to my house in the suburbs to try and get some sleep, though I doubted I would. That's when I got the text message on my phone. A message from Dalton.

IT ALL WOULD HAVE WORKED OUT FOR YOU, JACK, IF YOU'D ONLY GONE TO SEE MY SIS…

Looking at the word *SIS*, I realized what had been nagging at me, and I wanted to shoot myself for missing the obvious. On the back of the boy's picture, I'd assumed Dalton had written the number 515. But he hadn't written that. He'd written SIS.

I got on the radio to the watch commander back at my district and had her search for any of Dalton's relatives in the area.

"Anywhere specific?" she asked.

I thought about the photo I'd swiped from his condo, of the woman sitting on the porch.

"Schaumburg," I said.

Three minutes later, I was heading to Golf Road and Bode in the Northwest suburbs, going to visit Janice Dalton, John Dalton's younger sister. I called Herb en route, and he told me he'd meet me there. Maybe Janice knew something. Maybe the boy was still alive. I kept my foot on the gas, even without my siren, hoping against hope that we still had a chance.

After exiting onto Route 53, I got a call from the crime lab.

"Lieut, it's Hajek. My expert buddy looked at the photo and told me what was altered about it. It's not an original. It's a picture of picture, which has been colorized."

"Explain."

"These days, many photo studios can do photographic restoration. You know, fix scratches, rips, folds, fading. They can also add color to

old black and white photographs. That's what was done with the boy. It's a professional job, and we could probably trace who did the work."

"I'll get back to you."

I arrived at Janice Dalton's house—the same house as in the picture on Dalton's hallway wall—before Herb did. I knocked on her door without waiting for him.

Janice was older than I was, gray, with smile lines on her face that had deepened into serious wrinkles.

"Ms. Dalton, I'm Lieutenant Daniels from the police department. Do you know this person?"

I held up the boy's picture.

"Of course I do. That's my brother, John, when he was a kid. Is everything okay?"

I recalled Dalton's words, at the storage facility.

"I'm saying that we can only be here for so long. For some, it could be years before we leave. For others, it could be just over twenty-four and a half hours."

He hadn't been talking about a child's death. He was talking about a child leaving the country. And that child was him.

"Can I come in, Ms. Dalton?"

She nodded. I still wasn't sure why Dalton would send me on a wild goose chase. For fun? To prove he was smarter than I was? All of the books in his condo pointed to him being a true crime junkie. Maybe he just wanted to mess around with the famous cop he'd read about.

So what about all the innuendo? All the double-talk? Was Dalton even a criminal?

"Please, sit down. Would you like some coffee, Lieutenant? I can make a pot."

I plopped onto the sofa and stifled a yawn. "No, thank you. I just have a few questions about your brother. You know he left the country a little while ago?"

207

She nodded, sitting on the love seat. "A dream of his, to live on an island. He worked hard his whole life, saving up money. He finally earned enough to retire."

"What did your brother do?"

"Construction, I think. He never talked about his job. I know he made a lot of money. He helped me buy this house. You know, he told me, before he left, that someone would be stopping by here. He wanted me to give you something. Can you hold on just a moment?"

I nodded, tensing up. When Janice left the room, I reached into my blazer and unbuckled the strap on my shoulder holster, resting my hand on the butt of my Colt. But when she returned, it wasn't with a machine gun or a live grenade. It was with a notebook.

"I have no idea what this is," Janice said, handing the pad over.

It was a standard Mead school notebook, black cardstock cover, spiral bound, seventy pages. I flipped it open and saw it was filled with handwritten names and dates, starting in the 1970s.

I don't think my heart actually stopped, but that's what it felt like. Because I recognized some of those names. I began turning pages, and I watched as the dates progressed, over a hundred of them, eventually stopping two days ago. The date of the John Doe murder, the man who died on the Catherine Wheel.

This was Mr. K's murder book. A complete list of everyone he had killed.

I had just let history's biggest serial killer leave the country.

"Are you all right?" Janice asked me. "You just got a little pale."

I thanked her, excused myself, and managed to get out of there without having a complete and total nervous breakdown. Herb pulled up as I was walking to my Nova.

"Jack?" He hurried out of his car, his face awash with concern.

"Dalton was Mr. K," I said, handing Herb the notebook.

"You sure?"

I nodded. "The boy in the picture. It was him. He took us for a ride, Herb. And we let him."

Over twenty years on the force, and I'd never screwed up this big. I wanted to crawl into a hole and never come out again. When I thought about my life, about all I'd given up just to be a cop, I couldn't help but feel what a colossal waste it was. A failed marriage. No children. For what? What good were all the sacrifices I'd made, when the worst criminal in the history of the United States of America could play me like a cheap fiddle?

"Want to go get drunk?" Herb said.

"I want to go to Cape Verde, find the bastard, and blow his head off."

"But you won't."

I searched his face. "I won't?"

"You can break into an occasional home and hire scumbag private detectives to bend the law, but you're still a cop, Jack. It's in your blood, whether you like it or not. And because you're a cop, you're going to follow the rules. That's what you do. That's who you are. You know that. Which is why you know the good guys lose sometimes."

I stared up at the sun, which was so bright it hurt. Herb was right, or course. I didn't like it. Hell, I didn't like myself. Maybe, if I were a stronger person, I could fly to Dalton's little island paradise and snuff the murderous asshole.

But then again, if I were a stronger person, I probably should have quit the force years ago and started a family.

"Actually, getting drunk sounds pretty good right about now," I said. "You got the first round?"

"Absolutely. And just remember, Jack. Guys like Dalton, they don't just retire. I'd bet you a dozen donuts we haven't heard the last of him."

I stared at my partner and hoped he was right. Because if I ever got another shot at John Dalton, aka Mr. K, I wouldn't screw it up again.

Present day
2010, August 10

I opened my eyes and stared at John Dalton, aka Mr. K. The ball gag had been removed from my mouth, and my arms and legs were strapped to the Catherine Wheel. So was my waist, a tight canvas belt holding me to the circular plywood.

"Good. You're awake. I know you've been waiting a long time for this. I know I certainly have."

Dalton began to remove items from his bag and set them on the floor in front of me. A blow torch. A filet knife. A box of sea salt. And finally, a sledgehammer. He hefted the hammer, holding it before my face.

"Shall we get started, Jack?"

Twenty-one years ago
1989, August 17

I scrambled backward, away from Victor Brotsky, who loomed over me with a butcher knife. His naked body was blood-soaked, with bits of what must have been Shell sticking to his matted, curly hairs, covering him neck to toes.

In my effort to get away, I got tangled up—in Shell. I pushed away warm innards, which looped around my wrists, scooting over his dead body, off the plastic tarp, and over to the back door. It was locked, with a key-entry deadbolt, the same kind as the front door.

"Where you going to, little girl cop? There is no place to run from Victor Brotsky. My house is locked tight."

I reached for the cheap dinette set against the wall, picking up one of the kitchen chairs. It was rolled aluminum and flimsy pressboard, insubstantial, but I threw it with all that I had.

Brotsky batted it harmlessly away, like he was swatting a bothersome mosquito. I followed up with the other, matching chair, and then upended the brown, Formica table, using it as a shield.

"You are a fighter," Brotsky said. He grinned, exposing a cavern of yellow, crooked teeth. "I like. This is a fun job for me. Kill whores. Get paid. Now I get to kill pretty girlie cop. They pay me extra for you."

While I'd never fought for my life before, I had been in plenty of fights. I was a black belt, tae kwon do, and had been practicing the martial art since I was a girl. Squaring off against someone wasn't foreign to me—in fact, my forte was sparring. Even against a larger opponent, I was used to confrontation, and it didn't paralyze me.

Rather than try to control the fear, I used it, letting it fuel my muscles. When Brotsky stepped onto the tarp, I rushed him, leaping over Shell, lifting the table and ramming it into the knife. Brotsky hadn't been ready for the attack, and he stumbled backward, falling onto his backside. I rode the table over him, like a surfboard, the slashing blade missing me as I landed on my knees in the kitchen doorway.

I ran in a direction I hadn't gone before, hoping to find a weapon or an exit. Hurrying over the carpeted floor, I passed a bathroom—glass blocks on the window—and found a bedroom. I slammed the door behind me, pressing the cheap push-button lock, jumping onto Brotsky's unmade bed, and pulling back the drapes.

Another barred window.

Quickly looking around, I reached for the table lamp, which was made of brass and looked heavy. Next to the bed was one of those huge cellular radio phones, a Motorola Dyna-TAC. I reached for it, then, on the floor, I spotted something better.

My purse, on top of a pile of my clothes.

I reached for it, hoping my gun was still inside, dumping the contents onto the bed, grabbing my Beretta and jacking a round into the chamber just as the door burst inward.

I fired, missing as Brotsky threw himself at me. In a millisecond I adjusted my aim, squeezing the trigger a second time.

Nothing happened. My semi-automatic had jammed.

Then Brotsky was on top of me, swatting the gun away, his naked flesh pressing me down against the bed, his hands grabbing my wrist as his foul lips pressed hot against my ear.

"Now, *sooka*," he cooed, "we have some fun."

Present day
2010, August 10

Phineas Troutt was no stranger to being hit.

When he was diagnosed with cancer—cancer that doctors told him would be fatal—he decided to drop out of life. Instead of the rat race, he chose to live in the moment, on the fringe of society, taking what he wanted, when he wanted it. This began with robbing drug dealers and gangbangers, for the sole purpose of getting some quick cash to buy drugs and booze and whores to make him forget about the immediate physical pain, and the emotional pain, of a biological death sentence.

He'd done things, many things, he wasn't proud of, even though the people he hurt, for the most part, had it coming.

Brotsky had it coming. And if Phin had to endure a broken nose and a few cracked ribs in order to show Brotsky that evil didn't pay, he was willing to take his lumps.

But he hadn't expected Brotsky to be so strong. Or so savage.

The older man—he had to be in his sixties—was apparently releasing all the pent-up rage that had built up during his years of incarceration. He tackled Phin, driving him to the floor, pinning him down. Phin took a shot in the kidneys, then was smothered by Brotsky's flabby, sweaty neck, which smelled like powdered eggs.

Phin tried to heave the larger man off of him, but Brotsky was too big, too strong. Phin reached up, trying to scratch his eyes, but Brotsky craned his head back.

So Phin went for his nose. Making his index finger stiff, he jammed it into one of Victor Brotsky's flaring nostrils, up past the second knuckle, trying to drive it all the way to the bastard's brain.

Brotsky recoiled, pulling away, giving Phin the opportunity to slide out from under him.

Phin got onto his knees just as Brotsky rose to his feet. Roaring, snorting a clot of blood from his nose, Brotsky charged again. Phin timed the punch perfectly, catching Brotsky under the chin as he barreled toward him. The uppercut staggered the inmate, but didn't drop him. Phin followed up with a solid jab between the man's legs, but Brotsky twisted at the last moment, Phin's hand bouncing off his meaty thigh.

Phin dropped a shoulder and rolled left. Momentum carried him to the cot. He reached for it, pulling himself up on the frame, which was bolted to the floor, and turned around to face Brotsky.

So far, Phin's attempt to coerce the killer into a confession wasn't going too well.

"This cop," Brotsky said, wiping the back of his hairy paw against his bloody nose, "she is your girlfriend, yes?"

Jack was more than a girlfriend to Phin. In the sinkhole of chaos his life had become, Jack had been a constant, bright light. She was his friend, but also his ideal. To Phin, Jacqueline Daniels represented all that was good about humanity. Simply having her in his world was enough to kick Phin out of his dark depression and bring him back to the world of the living. She'd not only saved his life. She had also saved his soul.

"I love her," Phin said. This surprised him, because as close as he and Jack had been, he'd never said these words to her.

Now, facing the man who was responsible for abducting her, Phin realized he should have said them sooner. On one hand, he hadn't wanted to burden Jack with the responsibility of yet another man in her life. She'd had it rough lately, both personally and professionally. Phin didn't want to scare her away.

But he should have told her just the same. Jack didn't scare easily. And the mantra of their relationship—taking things one day at a time—had been exploded by the revelation that she was pregnant.

Not much scared Phin. But the thought that he'd never have a chance to tell the mother of his child how much he loved her was easily the most terrifying thing he'd ever endured.

"Did your woman tell you what Victor Brotsky did to her?" The prisoner grinned, blood running into his mouth and staining his crooked teeth red. "I hurt the sooka. I hurt her. *Real good.*"

Acting on anger, Phin threw himself at Brotsky. The larger man had anticipated the move, and his fist shot out, connecting with the side of Phin's head. Phin staggered to the side, his vision blurring, and then he dropped to his knees.

"And now," Victor Brotsky said, "I am going to hurt you. *Real good.*"

Twenty-one years ago
1989, August 17

Brotsky on top of me, sweating, grunting, crushing me with his obscene weight, was the most disgusting, horrifying feeling I'd ever experienced. It was even worse than him chasing me with the knife.

I felt his teeth on my neck, biting, harder than any lover would, his fat knees pushing against mine, forcing my legs apart.

Every instinct, every nerve in my body, screamed *FIGHT HIM!*

But I didn't.

Rapists liked the fighting back. Control and violence were part of the turn-on. Before joining Vice, I'd talked to a dozen streetwalkers in preparation for my undercover work. They had an almost universal response when johns got too violent.

Get the control back.

Obviously, I couldn't get control by fighting someone bigger and stronger. So I did it by confusing him.

Squeezing my eyes closed, fighting the urge to vomit, I made myself meet his clumsy kiss, pressing my lips to his. At the same time, I worked my free hand between our nude bodies, grasping him between the legs like I wanted him.

Brotsky's reaction was instantaneous, doing the same thing any man did when you grabbed his dumb-stick. He sighed, going lax. Then he kissed me back, his hand slipping around my waist, a guttural moan escaping his throat.

That's when I squeezed his balls with every intention of pulling them off.

Brotsky's groan became a high-pitched wail, and he wrapped his hand around my neck, cutting off my air, but in our little game, two balls beat one throat, and he let go and tried to roll off me, chopping at my wrists.

I released him, rolling off the other side of the bed, grabbing my dress as I hit the floor, beelining into the bathroom and slamming and locking the door behind me. I tugged the Versace over my head, feeling less vulnerable now that I was no longer naked, but my emotional state was a wreck. I was near hysterical, feeling like laughing and crying at the same time, amazed to have him off me, sick at what had happened so far, terrified at what was still going on.

I bit back the encroaching nervous breakdown and threw open the medicine cabinet, looking for a razor or scissors or anything sharp, listening to Brotsky howl in the bedroom, the howls getting louder as he came after me. There was nothing usable, so I spun around, searching for something. I saw towels, on a cheap rack. Brotsky's underwear and shoes, discarded on the floor. A basket in the corner, with a scrub brush and a roll of toilet paper.

I turned my attention to the toilet, grabbing the heavy porcelain lid on top of the tank, swinging it around just as Brotsky came barreling through the door.

The lid connected with his forehead, cracking in half, the impact hurting my fingers. Brotsky backpedaled, his arms pinwheeling as he fell onto his butt. I ran right at him, jumping over him as he fell.

Somehow, a nanosecond later, I wound up face-first on the carpet, bright stars blinding my vision from the impact.

Brotsky had grabbed my ankle. And he still had it.

I kicked out with my free leg, trying to drive my heel into some sensitive part of his body. But all I kept hitting was fat and flesh, my blows thudding off harmlessly. Then Brotsky turned, pinning my ankle, his weight forcing it into an unnatural position.

The *SNAP!* was loud enough for both of us to hear.

The pain was the worst thing I'd ever experienced.

Present day
2010, August 10

"Remember how it feels to break a bone, Jack?"

I blinked, my vision of John Dalton blurry. He was older, tanner, but the dead eyes and expressionless face were the same.

I swallowed. My wrists still burned, and my jaw ached. The ball gag was gone, but wearing it for so long had made my mouth tender.

"Is this you being the hero in the movie of your life, John?"

My voice sounded strange, echoey. A side effect of the drugs, I guessed.

"Ah, yes. I remember that conversation. That was my way of saying we're all very good at justifying our actions. But as for heroes...I'm afraid there are none. You're a perfect example of that. Dedicating your life to catching despicable villains. Giving up everything for your endless pursuit of evil. And where has all of that gotten you? Dying in agony."

Dalton moved closer, until we were almost cheek to cheek. "You're not a hero, Jack. You're an unhappy ending. A Greek

221

tragedy. An object lesson for those who try to lead a selfless life."

"You going to get on with this, Dalton?" I said through my clenched teeth. "Or are you going to talk me to death?"

Dalton took a step back, raising the sledgehammer.

"The leg first, I think," he said. "Which one did Victor Brotsky break? It was the right one, wasn't it?"

There was no way I could brace myself for it. So I didn't even try.

When the hammer connected with my tibia, cracking the bone, the pain was so bad that darkness overtook me.

Twenty-one years ago
1989, August 17

I'd heard the cliché *sharp pain* many times in my life, but that's exactly what it was when Brotsky snapped my leg— like someone was stabbing a skewer into my bone.

I jackknifed around, swiping at his eyes with my fingernails, getting him to let go of me. Then I crawled like crazy for the bedroom. Each time my knee hit the floor, the skewer dug deeper. My stomach felt like I'd swallowed a whirlpool, and my head got so light I could literally feel the blood draining from it. I went straight for the bed, pulling myself underneath the dust ruffle, waiting for Brotsky to come storming in.

But he didn't come storming in.

"I'll find you, *tee karova*! Victor Brotsky will find you!"

But his voice was further away than the bathroom. It sounded like he was coming from the kitchen.

Maybe, between the crack in the head and the scrape across the eyes, he hadn't seen where I'd gone.

Taking advantage of this, I peeked through the dust ruffle on my left side, looking for my gun.

Not there. I tried the right.

Also not there. But I did remember something that was there. Brotsky's gigantic cellular phone.

I inched closer to the side, gasping at the pain when my leg was jostled. The gasp filled my mouth with a giant dust bunny, sticking in the back of my throat. I slapped my hand over my mouth so I didn't cough.

"Where are you, sooka?"

Brotsky was closer now. Maybe in the hallway. My lungs spasmed, but I wouldn't let the air out.

"Did you go back downstairs, to play with Brotsky's collection?"

I heard his feet creaking on the basement steps. Now was the time to act. Inch by painful inch, I dragged myself out from under the bed, pulling my broken leg behind me.

Above me, on the nightstand, was the Motorola Dyna-TAC. The pain was becoming so bad I was going to either scream or pass out, and I didn't see any way I'd be able to sit up and grab the phone. So, from a prone position, I reached for it, stretching my hand up, brushing it with the tips of my fingers.

The stairs creaked again, getting louder. Brotsky was coming back up.

I strained, grunting with effort, pinching the base of the phone between my thumb and forefinger.

Brotsky's footsteps, in the hallway.

Finally getting a firm grip, I pulled the phone from the nightstand. It was heavy, about two pounds, eighteen inches long with the antenna. I shoved it under the bed, then pushed myself backward, trying to get under the dust ruffle before Brotsky came back.

Holding my breath, I listened for the killer.

I didn't hear anything. Not a single sound.

Turning my attention to the phone, I pressed one of the buttons. The keypad lit up, bright green.

Still no noises from Brotsky.

I tapped a number, the beep so loud it made me flinch. The red LED screen displayed a digital number 9. Sure Brotsky must have heard it, I tapped 1 and 1 again, waiting for the operator to pick up, hoping they didn't put me on hold.

It rang.

And rang.

And rang.

Then they put me on hold.

I could feel my leg throb with my heartbeat. I had no idea how serious the break was, but there was no way I'd be able to get out of there without assistance. If they didn't pick up soon...

"Nine one one, what is the nature of your emergency?"

The connection wasn't the best, and the operator's words fluctuated in volume. "This is Officer Jacqueline Streng," I whispered. "I'm in a house with a killer. There are eleven dead, possibly more. His name is Victor Brotsky."

"Where are you located, Officer?"

"I don't know. Can't you pinpoint the call?"

"We can't. Are you using a land line at the location?"

I forced myself not to yell. "Goddamn it, just look up his goddamn address."

"I'm looking it up, Officer. But I don't have any Chicago addresses for Victor Protsy."

Goddamn bad reception. "His name isn't Protsy. It's—"

Then the mattress and box spring were lifted off the frame and tossed aside, and Brotsky was reaching down for me, a sharpened broom handle clenched in his meaty fist.

Present day
2010, August 10

On his knees, Phin looked up at the bear of a man eagerly approaching. Lust sparkled in Brotsky's bulging eyes, and his clenched fists were the size of hams and ready to serve up more damage. Dizzy from Brotsky's last punch, weak from the chemotherapy, Phin realized he wasn't only going to lose the fight, but he'd probably be killed as well.

Sorry, Jack. You deserved so much better.

Then Victor Brotsky halted in mid-step, his whole body vibrating. His mouth opened, and he dropped like a redwood tree, his spine ramrod stiff, the two thin, silver wires sticking out of his chest trailing a small puff of smoke. Phin heard a crackling discharge of electricity, then followed the wires and turned to see—

—Harry McGlade, standing in the doorway, holding a taser gun.

"I bribed the warden ten grand to watch you get your ass kicked," Harry said, "and now just blew another K on the guard's taser. Find out where Jack is."

Phin didn't hesitate. He leapt onto Brotsky, sweeping away the electrodes, pinching the man's chubby neck.

"Where?" he demanded.

"Da?"

He squeezed harder, seeking Brotsky's trachea through the flab. "Where is she!"

"Meester K has her. He…is going to kill her."

Phin slapped the confused Brotsky across the face. The killer smelled of stale sweat and ozone, and his eyes weren't focused. "Where does he have her, Victor?"

Brotsky stared up at Phin, his expression almost childlike in its honesty. "I don't know. The man I hired, he did not tell me."

If Phin had had a gun, or a knife, he would have killed the fat bastard right then and there. Because he believed Brotsky was telling the truth. Jack was about to die, and there was no way to save her.

He focused more pressure on Brotsky's neck, his forearms straining, his fingers cramping. Putting all of his fear and anger into it. Thinking that if Jack were going to die, this piece of shit would precede her.

Brotsky's eyes bugged out and his tongue began to protrude. He tried to reach for Phin, but the smaller man had pinned the killer's arms with his knees.

"If there's a hell," Phin said through clenched teeth as he watched the life drain out of Brotsky, "I'll see you there, so I can kill you again."

Then Brotsky tried to say something. A glimmer of hope overtook Phin. Did the killer know something after all? Phin let up the pressure enough to allow Brotsky to speak.

"C-c-call…her," the fat man sputtered.

Call her? That actually made sense. The camera over Jack was connected to an iPhone. Perhaps it was possible to talk to the guy who had Jack. Make some kind of deal.

"What's the number?" Phin demanded, relaxing his trembling hands.

Brotsky coughed. "I do not know. But Meester K will call me. He said he would. I paid him to. He sent me the phone so I could watch her die, and hear her screams."

Then Phin heard it. Music, coming from the hallway. It was Garth Brooks, "Friends in Low Places." Phin released Brotsky, ran past the guards who'd been watching with casual interest, and saw Herb sitting with his back against the wall, staring at the iPhone as it played the country tune—Brotsky's ringtone.

Herb's jowls were slick, tear-stained, his eyes rimmed in red.

"Dalton...he...broke her leg..."

Phin snatched the phone from Herb, running his finger along the touch screen to answer it.

"Is this Dalton?" Phin was surprised how calm and together he managed to sound.

"Who is this?" a man answered.

There was no point in lying. "My name is Phineas Troutt. I was in bed next to Jack when you grabbed her."

"Ah, yes. You must be the father of the baby. Would you like to talk to the mother? I'll try to wake her up for you."

Phin held the iPhone away from his face, seeing Jack on the wheel, seeing Mr. K wave something under her face—smelling salts—waking her up.

Jack's face transformed from the peace of sleep to a mask of twisted agony. Something inside Phin snapped. He slid to the floor, next to Herb, his own tears coming fast and hard.

"Jack?" Phin's voice was thick, the words threatening to clog up his throat. "Where are you, babe?"

"Phin? Is that you?" Jack's voice was strained, her breath labored.

"It's me." He pressed the screen, putting it on speaker phone. "Do you know where you are?"

"No. I'm...I'm with a man named John Dalton. Herb...he knows who he is."

Dalton? Phin had no idea who he was. He'd been expecting Luther Kite.

Then Phin realized Luther Kite couldn't have been the one to grab Jack, because there had been no nettles in the house. When Phin came down from the tree where Kite had been, he'd gotten covered in nettles, and had dragged them into the kitchen. If Luther had been in the house, he'd have done the same.

Phin heard a scream coming from Brotsky's cell. Then the guards rushed in. "Herb's here with me. So's Harry."

"I'm here, Jack," Herb said, leaning close. A tear slid down his nose, splashing onto the phone. "I'm so sorry. I'm so, so sorry."

"It's not your fault, Herb. Nothing you could have done."

"Jack..." Herb began to cry so badly he couldn't talk. The cop pressed his hand over his face and began to shake. More guards hurried up the hall, piling into Brotsky's cell.

Jack looked up at the camera. *"You're my best friend, Herb. And you're the best man I've ever met. It was such an honor to work with you, to know you, for all of these years."*

"You're my best friend too, Jack. I...love you."

Jack's tortured face broke into a sad smile. *"And you didn't even have to be drunk to say it. I love you too, buddy."*

Harry walked over and crouched down. His hands were bloody, and his expression grim.

"Jackie? Can you hear me? It's me, Harry."

Jack nodded, her head slumping down as her body shook with sobs.

"Victory Brotsky, he said he paid to watch you die," Harry said, his voice cracking. "But he won't, Jack. He won't watch anything ever again, because I just poked his fucking eyes out."

"Thanks, Harry. Tell Mom I love her, would you? And take care of her for me?"

"I will, Jack." Now Harry started to cry. "And I know I've been an asshole. A huge asshole."

"You're my favorite asshole on the planet, Harry McGlade."

"And you're…the bravest person I've ever known, Jackie Daniels."

"You and Phin are going to hunt down this bastard for me, right?"

Harry nodded. "There won't be a place on earth he can hide from us."

"Phin?" Jack began to cry.

"I'm right here, babe."

Jack hung her head down, then summoned some inner reserve of courage and looked up into the camera. Right at Phin.

"I'm pregnant."

Phin struggled to control his own sob. "I know."

"I was thinking. If it was going to be a girl, to name her after my mother. If it was a boy…oh, Christ…if it was a boy…" Jack stuck out her lower jaw, defiant and strong. *"I want to name it after you guys. The men in my life. Phineas Herbert Harrison Daniels."*

Phin shook his head. "I'm sorry, babe. But you got the names wrong. If it's a boy, or a girl, we have to name it after the woman I love. Jack. Our child has to be named Jack. I love you so much."

"I love you too, Phin. That's why I've got a last request."

Phin had to wipe away the tears, because he couldn't see anything but blurs. "Name it."

Jack stared up at the camera again. *"Don't watch me die."*

"Jack..."

"Please. It will hurt more if I know you're watching. Promise me."

Phin summoned up the courage to lie to her. "I promise, Jack. We won't watch. I love you."

"I love—"

Dalton took the phone away, holding it to his ear. *"That was touching. Really. Now I've got a proposition for you gentlemen. I want a hundred thousand dollars, wired to my account."*

Phin's spirit soared. Was this guy actually going to let her live?

"A hundred grand, and you let Jack go?" Herb asked.

"Don't be silly. Jack is going to die today. I'm planning on breaking her legs and her arms, ripping her child from her womb, spinning her on the wheel, then pulling out her intestines, inch by inch." Dalton looked up at the camera. *"But if you wire me the money, I'll be merciful and put a bullet in her head right now."*

Twenty-one years ago
1989, August 17

The Motorola DynaTAC cellular phone was an expensive, state-of-the-art communications device on the cutting edge of technology. It also weighed about two pounds and was shaped like a brick.

It hit with the force of a brick, too, when I smashed it into Victor Brotsky's forehead as he pulled away the box spring and mattress and reached for me.

The fat psychopath dropped to his knees, stunned, blood erupting from the goose-egg on his head. I'd managed to hit him in the same spot I'd whacked him with the toilet. Figuring three times is a charm, I did it once more.

The phone held up surprisingly well. Brotsky, on the other hand, did not. His eyelids fluttered and he fell forward, crushing me under his elephantine weight.

The sudden pressure on my leg also pushed me to the brink of consciousness. Pushing, hard as I could, I leveraged him off me and he rolled onto his side. Then I crawled out from under the metal bed frame. I still didn't see my gun, and now the mattress and box spring were covering most of the bedroom floor. But I was able to locate some of the contents of my purse, including my police-issue handcuffs.

Staring back at Brotsky, who had begun to snore, I knew cuffing him was the best move. But every instinct I had told me to get the hell out of there, get away. It was a moment right out of every bad horror movie. The psycho is knocked out, and the heroine runs rather than finishing him off.

Killing Brotsky wasn't an option for me. I was a cop, and I respected the law. Every part of the law. Too many older cops I knew bent rules and broke laws in the course of their jobs, and I was determined to never let that happen to me. Besides, killing a helpless, unarmed human being, cop or no cop, was something I knew I'd never be able to do.

But cuff him? Absolutely, I should cuff him.

Now all I needed was the guts to do it.

Mark Twain once said that true bravery isn't the absence of fear, but the ability to act in the face of fear. I was certainly experiencing fear at that moment. Fear, pain, exhaustion, disgust, and myriad other emotions, none of them pleasant.

So this was my chance to be brave.

Clutching my handcuffs like they were a talisman, I dragged myself back to Victor Brotsky. The closer I got, the more I thought of another horror film cliché. The one where the killer suddenly opens his eyes and grabs the victim.

When I finally reached Brotsky, I tried as hard as I could, but I couldn't force myself to grab his wrist. The image of him, naked and writhing on top of me, threatened to make me physically ill, and my hands were shaking so bad the cuffs were rattling.

But that moment, that test, was the reason I had become a police officer. I joined the force to catch bad guys. Real bad guys, not the pathetic idiots paying street hookers for BJs.

Victor Brotsky was as bad as they got. And if I didn't have the guts to do this, I had no business being a cop.

My teeth had begun to chatter from fear, but I managed to get a cuff open and snick it around Brotsky's fat wrist.

That's when he stopped snoring.

Moving quickly, I pulled on his arm, forcing it behind him, looping the chain around the metal support beam in the center of the bed frame. Then I reached for his other hand.

He was lying on it, pinning it beneath his massive bulk. I dug my fingers under him, breaking out in goosebumps at the touch of his moist, warm flab.

Brotsky groaned, shifting his weight, exposing his free wrist. I yanked on the cuffs, desperately trying to get the chain to reach.

Then he turned his fat head and opened his eyes, staring right at me.

I felt myself pucker in horror, and the adrenaline surge gave me just enough strength to pull the cuff that extra inch and lock it around the monster's other hand.

I jerked away from him as he suddenly sat up, jostling the bed frame. His shoulders flexed, his hairy fat jiggling as he erupted with a string of Russian words that I didn't understand, but was pretty sure weren't flattering. On my butt, I pushed myself away with my good leg, while Brotsky tried to get up on his knees and come after me. But his position, and the bed frame, kept him in place.

Red-faced, flecks of foamy spittle flying from his screaming mouth, he finally said something I understood.

"I WILL KILL YOU, YOU FILTHY COP WHORE!"

I'd been threatened by a lot of perps, but none sounded as wholly convincing. The pure hate and rage made me want to shrink into a ball and hide.

Which is why I stuck out my chin, defiant.

"You're going to prison forever, asshole. Your killing days are over."

Brotsky roared, quaking with fury. I backed the hell away from him, scooting my way to the bedroom door. My leg still throbbed with my heartbeat, but strangely, it seemed more bearable.

Once in the hallway, I turned to face my new nemesis: the phone on the wall. The receiver was still hanging on its cord from when I'd dropped it. Moving slowly, the carpeting warm under my butt, I made my way toward it as Brotsky continued to thrash and scream, his efforts making the floor shake.

I reached the phone, putting the receiver to my ear. The line was dead. There wasn't even that annoying, off-the-hook beeping.

I knew what I had to do—stand up, hit the bar to get a dial tone, and call 911 again.

Putting my back against the hallway wall, I pressed both palms against it, then pulled my good knee to my chest. My injured leg was swollen, like someone had inflated it with an air pump, but it didn't look bent or misshapen. Perhaps the break wasn't as bad as it felt.

Pushing hard, flexing my healthy leg, lifting with my hands, I was able to shimmy up the wall and balance on one foot. Beads of sweat had sprung out of every pore on my body, and I closed my eyes and controlled my breathing and slowed my heart rate in an effort to keep from passing out.

Brotsky continued to rage in the bedroom, and the clanging of the metal bed frame against the floor sounded like he was tearing it to pieces. I turned my attention to the phone, reeling in the receiver on its curly cord, tapping the disconnect cradle a few times, getting a dial tone, sticking my finger in the 9 of the wheel—

—just as Victor Brotsky filled the bedroom doorway.

I dialed 9, hands trembling, thinking about how easy it was to screw up a number on these phones, and how it took forever to dial again. I couldn't afford to make a mistake.

Brotsky thrashed, trying to force himself into the hall, but the bed frame was too big and wouldn't pull through.

I stuck my finger in the 1 and spun the dial again. The rotary seemed to turn in slow motion, taking forever for the *click-click-click-click* to get to 0.

Brotsky spat more invectives at me in several languages. He managed to get his shoulders through the door, but the frame still held him at bay.

My finger found the last 1, the dial taking impossibly, ridiculously long to register the number, and then, blessedly, I heard ringing on the other end.

Brotsky bellowed, more animal than human. His head shook, his shoulders straining, and then there was a tiny, almost insignificant *ching* sound.

His hands came free, and Brotsky stumbled forward.

He had broken the handcuffs.

Present day
2010, August 10

"*Jack,*" Phin said as Dalton held his phone to my face. I could hear the pain in Phin's voice, and my heart bled for him. "*What do you want us to do?*"

My leg throbbed, and every tiny jiggle of the wheel I was strapped to brought waves of agony. I couldn't imagine having all of my limbs broken, then spun. It would be unendurable.

But then I thought of a Mark Twain quote. The one about bravery in the face of fear. It was a truism that had served me well throughout my life, prompting me to do things I never thought I was capable of doing.

Yes, I'd made mistakes. Yes, I'd missed some opportunities.

But I really did believe I'd made the world a slightly better place, because of my efforts. Trying to objectively judge my years on this planet, I figured I deserved that B+ as a final grade.

An A- would be sweeter, though. And last words, last acts, if they were brave enough, could perhaps count for a bit of extra credit and make my time here just a little bit more worthwhile.

I'd never been big on spirituality. I had no illusions that this life would lead to another.

That meant, for every second I still breathed, I had to make this life count.

If my final act could be one of defiance, of bravery, or showing fear that it had no hold over me, then I damn well earned that A-.

I looked at John Dalton—Mr. K—dead in the face and spoke evenly, clearly, and calmly to Phin—no tears, no regrets, no hint of fear, knowing these might well be my last words.

"Don't give this prick a dime."

Twenty-one years ago
1989, August 17

"This is Officer Jacqueline Streng!" I yelled, dropping the receiver and hopping away from the phone as Brotsky rushed at me. "Officer needs assistance! Officer needs fucking assistance!"

I limped backward as Brotsky charged like a bull, panic overriding my pain. He would be on me any second, and I had two choices of where to go: the basement, or the kitchen.

I threw myself into the kitchen, climbing over the upside-down table, belly-flopping over Shell's cooling corpse, scrambling for the utensil drawer in the cabinet. My fingers sought, and found, the handle, and I jerked my arm back, silverware exploding into the air and raining down on me, the tarp, the counter.

Locking my hand around a steak knife, I twisted onto my back and faced Brotsky's attack, my weapon outstretched and clenched in a death grip.

But Victor Brotsky wasn't there.

Still brandishing the knife, I felt behind me for the counter, painfully pulling myself up to my good foot while wondering where he'd gone. My imagination fired into overdrive, conjuring up scenarios. Was he going to get a gun? Had he heard me calling the police and fled the house? Or was he on the phone with someone, maybe the person he'd been talking to earlier?

"I'll take care of her soon," he had said. *"In fact, I'll do it right now."*

What if Victor Brotsky was calling for backup?

I needed to get the hell out of there. Right now.

Keeping one eye on the doorway, I began tugging open drawers, looking for keys. The back door was right behind me. If I found the damn deadbolt key, I was sure I'd get to safety, because once I had an out, I would break the world record for the hundred yard dash, even if I had a compound fracture.

The drawers contained more utensils, loose change, various plastic toys from cereal boxes, bendy straws, pens and pencils, and an assortment of maps. But no keys.

Expanding my search, I began opening cabinets. Plates, glassware, plastic containers, pots and pans, but nothing else. No key hooks on the walls. No key bowl on the counter. I hadn't noticed any keys in the bedroom, or the bathroom. And he was naked, so he certainly didn't have them on him.

So where were they? Men don't have purses, so where did they put their goddamn keys? Their pants?

Could the keys be in Brotsky's pants?

I pictured him taking off his clothes so they wouldn't get bloody when he murdered Shell. Brotsky excited. In a hurry. He might very well leave his keys in his front pocket while he undressed.

I tried to envision the bedroom. I'd seen my clothes in there. But had Brotsky's been in there, too? On the bed? On the floor?

The bathroom! I'd stepped over his stained underwear in the bathroom.

Though my pulse was still pumping like a thrash metal song, the adrenaline in my system had faded enough for the pain to become debilitating. With one hand on the counter-top, I hopped once toward the kitchen entryway. The exquisite agony that shot through me literally pushed tears right out of my eyes.

How many more hops to the bathroom? Fifteen? Twenty? Then twenty back?

Crawling, or scooting, would hurt less, but take longer. Any second, Brotsky might make an appearance. Speed was paramount.

I scooped up a wooden spoon from one of the open drawers, jammed the handle in my mouth, and ground my molars on it as I hopped for the door.

Keeping quiet wasn't a concern anymore. Whimpers soon became cries. Cries became deep moans. Then moans turned into full-wattage screams. Halfway into the hall, my entire world had been reduced to the incessant throb in my tortured leg and my raw throat, which ached like my vocal chords were bleeding.

When I reached the bathroom, throwing my hand on the doorframe, I almost wept in relief.

But my relief was short-lived.

Victor Brotsky was standing next to the bathroom sink, zipping up his pants.

Present day

2010, August 10

Dalton stares back at Jack with mild surprise. He knows
he gave her leg a solid hit, and that the bone snapped.
Not too many people could remain cool in the grip of such
pain.

He puts the phone to his ear and speaks to Phin, Jack's
boyfriend.

"What is it you'd like to do?"

There is silence.

"While you're deciding, I'd be happy to break her other
leg."

"We'll pay," Phin says. *"Just don't hurt her anymore."*

Dalton's mouth twitches in a slight smile. "Get something to write with. I'm going to give you a routing number.
Then you'll have ten minutes to transfer the money into my
account."

"Phin! Don't give him—!"

Dalton gives Jack a swift kick in her shattered shin,
prompting a scream.

"Shh," Dalton tells her. "It's rude to interrupt."

"Stop hurting her, you son of a bitch!"

"Here's the number." Dalton rattles off the digits and hangs up. "Luckily, your friends have more sense than you do, Jack. They're going to pay."

Jack says nothing. Dalton can't tell if she's upset or relieved. Either way, he doesn't care.

Dalton is tired. He flew into North America through Canada, under a fake name, and has been working nonstop since his arrival. That Brotsky somehow was able to get in touch was a big surprise. But the crazy Russian had been a standup guy in jail, not naming names, keeping his mouth shut. When he inherited that money, Dalton's former employer had contacted him on Brotsky's behalf, keeping a generous finder's fee.

At first, Dalton hadn't wanted to take this job. He was getting old. But after three years of retirement, he was grateful for a change of scenery and the chance to stretch his old muscles.

Besides, the opportunity to torture the legendary Jack Daniels to death was something he really couldn't pass up. Two very distinguished careers were coming to an end with this single moment.

After he'd given Jack his murder notebook, via his sister Janice, the U.S. had gone Mr. K crazy. There had been two different TV movies, a Hollywood feature staring James Woods, half a dozen books, and a gangsta rapper had a #3 Billboard hit called "Do the Dalton." It had been great fun, and Dalton wouldn't mind seeing a resurgence in his popularity when Jack's broken body was discovered and the video of her agonizing death showed up on YouTube.

And her death would be agonizing. Right after the wire transfer went through, Dalton was going to break the rest of Jack's limbs, just for starters.

It is a serendipitous turn of events that her friends and lover are watching. Now they'll get to witness Jack's suffering, while also being out a hundred thousand dollars. It's so delightfully horrible that James Woods will be drooling to do the sequel.

Yes, this is certainly worth coming out of retirement for.

Twenty-one years ago
1989, August 17

Seeing Victor Brotsky, standing in the bathroom within arm's reach, flipped a switch in me. I knew it was a turning point. Whatever I did next would shape the rest of my life.

If I ran, I was also running away from this career. And it would have made perfect sense to run. I'd witnessed more horror in the last hour than most had in their entire lives. I could picture life with Alan, being a housewife, having children, never having to deal with crime or murder or psychos ever again.

That scenario certainly had a lot of appeal.

But there was another side to that coin. Instead of running, I could attack. If I did that, I saw the life I always wanted, living it as the woman I wanted to be. A Homicide cop. A police lieutenant. Someone that others would respect. Admire. Look up to.

Either way, I was probably going to die.

But it mattered to me whether I died running, or died fighting.

Brotsky and I stared at each other. It was probably for no more than a second, but it seemed much longer. Long enough for me to make a decision. Long enough for me to decide what I wanted out of life.

There was a *SNAP.*

The spoon in my teeth. I'd bitten the wood handle in half.

Then I launched myself at the son of a bitch.

Brotsky's eyes went wide. He raised up his hands in a defensive position as I hopped forward, stabbing at him with the steak knife, hearing a snarl that I recognized was my voice. I cut his forearm, his shoulder, and then buried the blade half-way into his flabby chest.

He slapped me, catching me on the chin, and I went sprawling out into the hallway. My back hit the wall so hard I saw stars. But I managed to keep my balance and keep hold of the knife.

Brotsky stared at me. The craziness was still there, in his eyes, but so was something else.

Fear. He was afraid of me.

"Come on, you chicken shit!" I screamed at him, waving the knife in front of me, the serrated blade dripping with his blood.

Victor Brotsky dug his hand into his pocket.

He pulled out his keys.

Then he ran past me, heading for the front door.

Five seconds later, he had it open.

Five seconds after that, he was on his knees, hands behind his head, as three cops covered him and three more ran inside, guns out, bathed in blinking red and blue lights from the half dozen squad cars parked on the street, the lawn, and on Victor Brotsky's violet garden.

Present day
2010, August 10

"You're going to torture me, even if you get the money," I told John Dalton.

He stared at me, saying nothing. Though my leg hurt so badly I feared I was going to go crazy, I managed to bark out a laugh.

"You're pathetic, John. You think you're so special. Emotionless. An iceman. You kill only because you're good at it. Because it pays well. But I see through your lies. I know your real secret."

Dalton's eyes narrowed, but he stayed quiet.

"What was that bullshit you told me, years ago? About the two types of killers. The one who got off on evil acts, and the other who had no passion for it. No emotion. You were trying to tell me that was you. The cold, emotionless one. What an epic denial." I leaned forward, stretching against my bonds. "But you're not emotionless at all, are you, John? You love this shit. I can picture you, in your mansion on the beach, watching your movies, reading your books, getting all hot and

247

bothered and jerking off to the sick things you've done to people."

This time, he actually flinched. The cold, hard mask of his face began to fall away.

"Oh, wait a minute. It wasn't just the books, was it? Your kink is photography. That's your porn, isn't it, John? I bet you've got a whole stash of photos, of all the sick shit you did to people. Is that the only way you can feel like a man? By hurting the helpless?"

Dalton folded his arms across his chest and began to chew on his lower lip. "I did it for the money."

"You did it because it gets you off. You know I'm right. You can't wait to use that speculum on me, can you? I bet you got really turned on when you bought that. Tell me something, Mr. K. How many of your victims did you rape?"

"I...I didn't rape any of them."

"You don't sound convinced, John. I'm betting you did rape them. You were careful. Used protection. Knew the only way you'd ever get laid is if you had someone tied up, at your mercy. Or maybe you were so afraid of leaving evidence that you just masturbated into your handkerchief while they were in agony." I watched his face, saw I'd hit home with that last one. "Yeah, that's it, isn't it? You weren't even man enough to fuck them. You're too pathetic for that."

Dalton shook his head. His left eye had begun to tic.

"I know you, John. This was never just a job to you. This is your kink. Your sick fetish. You're not some cool as ice hit man. You're a pervert. A sexual deviant. A sadist. No different than any of the other trash who came before you. No different than Brotsky. You wear expensive suits. Drive a Caddy. Get paid to live out your pathetic little fantasies. But you're just a regular, by-the-book psychopath. Textbook DSM-IV.

What was the trigger, Johnny Boy? Were you one of those little freaks who liked breaking their pet hamster's legs? Setting fires? I bet you wet the bed until you were fifteen."

Dalton blushed and turned away. I saw blood in the water, and went for it.

"What happened to you, John? Did Daddy get drunk and smack you around? Did Father O'Malley get a little too grabby when you were in Sunday school? Or was it your sister, Janice? Did she do bad things to Little Johnny when the lights went out?"

Then he was on me, hands at my throat, shaking my whole body. Gone was the calculated veneer, the façade he'd spent his whole life trying to portray. Instead, he was just another drooling, raging sexual predator. A dime a dozen. Pathetic. I'd dealt with so many of them it was almost passé to be killed by one.

I began to see spots, and darkness crept into my peripheral vision. But I wasn't afraid. In fact, in a way, I'd won. My plan had worked. Instead of my death being dragged out for hours, he was going to kill me immediately. In just a few words, I'd picked apart his psyche and reduced him to the animal he really was.

I could die now.

Die knowing Phin and Harry and Herb would avenge me.

Die with the knowledge of having lived the life I wanted to live.

Die the way I chose to, with dignity and bravery and victory.

The door to the storage locker burst open, and a tall, pale man with long, black hair rushed up to Dalton and pressed a stun gun into his neck.

Mr. K's eyes bugged out, and he collapsed into a pile. My rescuer jolted him again, making him dance and twitch.

Then again.

And again.

And again.

And again.

Dalton convulsed, spitting foam, his body contorting and twisting into odd positions. Eventually his eyes rolled up into his head, and he was still, save for the steady rise and fall of his chest.

The pale man looked at me. He wore a black turtle-neck sweater and blue work pants. His gaze was relaxed, but focused. Like I was being studied.

"You're Lieutenant Jack Daniels of the Chicago Police Department, responsible for catching more serial killers than any other law enforcement officer in history."

I coughed. Blinked. Nodded.

"Do you know who I am, Jack?"

I didn't. And then I did. I remembered the case. The crimes. The photograph the Wal-Mart security camera had captured of him seven years ago during his killing spree across North Carolina—the only photograph in any law enforcement database of this monster.

"You're Luther Kite," I said.

He leaned in, close enough to kiss. I forced myself not to flinch, meeting his stare while also knowing the situation hadn't changed. I'd simply swapped one maniac for another. But there was something different about this one. All my life, I'd wondered about true evil. I didn't wonder anymore, because I was staring into its black, soulless eyes.

"I've been watching you for a long time, Jack."

Luther's breath was sour. His skin smelled like Windex.

"Why have you been watching me, Luther?"

"Because I find you—" Luther stuck out a tongue the color of rotten liver, and licked my cheek "—interesting."

I tried not to gag and said, "What is it you want from me, Luther?"

"You're hurt." He glanced down at the floor, bent over, lifted something Dalton had dropped. The pregnancy test. "Hurt, and...with child. How far along are you?"

"A month," I said. A moment ago, I thought I'd conquered my fear. But it was coming back, with bells on.

"A month," Luther said, nodding. "It must be indescribably beautiful to have a life growing inside you."

"It is," I said. I managed to keep my voice even, but I could feel the tears coming.

Luther reached out, touching my thigh. His hand lingered, ice cold, then trailed upward. When he reached my belly, he rested his palm there and stared into my eyes.

"I couldn't let this man kill you, Jack. He isn't worthy. Didn't even notice I was watching him. Such an amateur. Do you know him?"

"He's Mr. K."

Luther's black eyes sparkled, and he took his horrible hand away from me. "*The* Mr. K?"

I nodded. Luther disappeared, walking behind me. A moment later, the Catherine Wheel was being lowered to the ground, and I was on my back. Luther crawled over, kneeling between my legs. Again, he brought his face within kissing distance. But instead of licking me again, he sniffed me. My nose. My lips. My neck. Every time he moved in, my skin shrank away from him.

Then he was down by my feet, unbuckling my ankle restraints.

"It's a bad break," he said. "But this should help."

I felt a pinch on my thigh, like a bee sting.

A moment later, the world became a warm, loving blanket. Pain free and fuzzy and euphoric.

I watched Luther put the syringe back into his pocket. Then he freed the strap around my waist, around my wrists. I threw a punch at him, but my swing was so slow, so weak. He easily dodged it, and then he had my wrists in his hands and I heard a *ZZZZZZ* sound. I looked down, saw a plastic zip tie securing my wrists.

"Don't try to run away," Luther said. "You'll make your leg worse."

He gave my broken bone a pat, which caused a bolt of agony to shoot through me and quickly vanish. I looked down, saw my foot bent in an odd direction. It looked really painful. I felt bad for whoever had such a terrible injury.

Luther dragged me by my armpits over to the concrete block. I sat there, watching, as he pulled Mr. K onto the Catherine Wheel and began buckling him on. Then he frisked him.

"What did you give me?" I asked, feeling so light I was worried I'd float away.

"Heroin. Good, isn't it?"

It was good. But it was also scary. I needed to get away from there. I tried to get up, but my leg bent a funny way and I fell over.

"You really need to sit still, Jack," Luther said. He was standing above me, holding Mr. K's sledgehammer.

Then there was screaming. A lot of screaming. Begging and screaming and more screaming until I had to put my hands over my ears, but I couldn't because someone had tied them up.

"Would you like a turn?" Luther asked, holding out the hammer for me.

I saw Mr. K, upside down on the Catherine Wheel. He was in bad shape. His legs and arms didn't even look like legs and

arms anymore. Luther gave the wheel a spin, and the screaming went on and on.

"No," I said, shrinking away. I didn't like any of this. I just
wanted to go home.

"He hurt you. This is your chance to hurt him back."

Luther pressed the sledgehammer handle into my bound
hands. I swung at Luther, but again I was too slow, missing by
a mile. Luther shook his head, taking the hammer away.

"Your loss."

Then he went to Mr. K again. He was doing something to
him with a knife.

Oh God.

The Guinea Worm.

Luther managed to get it going, and set them both so they
turned by themselves. He had to stand right next to Mr. K and
keep waving smelling salts in front of him, because Dalton
kept passing out.

After a long time, the smelling salts stopped working.

Luther sat down next to me, throwing the ammonia vial
across the floor.

"For a legend, he was a real disappointment," Luther said.
Then he turned to me. "I hope you don't turn out to be a disappointment, Jack."

Then I was on my back, Luther over me, pressing his lips
to my forehead.

"I'll be seeing you," he whispered. "Soon."

He pushed something into my hand. Dalton's phone.

A moment later, he was gone.

Twenty-one years ago
1989, August 19

I didn't get the credit for Brotsky's collar. That went to the six cops who burst into his house. Even though I'd cuffed Brotsky, I hadn't actually placed him under arrest, or read him his rights.

Brotsky offered up a full confession, and he gleefully blabbed about all of the atrocities he had committed. But he kept a few key facts to himself. Though he claimed that he had been hired by the Outfit, he never mentioned anyone by name. According to him, he slaughtered one of their high-class escorts, and they sent a hit man to his house. But rather than kill him, the hit man hired him to keep eliminating escorts, but to make sure they were the competition, not the ones owned by the Mafia. When pressed if this hit man was the elusive figure known as Mr. K, Brotsky just smiled.

When Brotsky had grabbed me and Shell, I hadn't been his original target. Shell had been. He'd been following Shell, and had gotten in line behind us—something I vaguely recalled—at Buddy Guy's, drugging our drinks while they languished on the bar. When Brotsky found out I was a cop after searching my purse, he was ordered to murder me as well.

Though Herb saw me get into Shell's car, he never heard that we went to Buddy Guy's instead of Miller's. Herb had spent three hours at Miller's, waiting for us, when he caught the squeal about me and Brotsky on the radio. Herb got to the scene a little after the uniforms had arrived. He rode in the ambulance with me.

"You are one helluva cop," he said as they were putting the cast on my leg. "When are you going to take your detective's exam?"

"Soon," I promised.

"Still interested in Homicide?"

"Absolutely."

Herb smiled widely and shook his head. "One helluva cop, Jacqueline."

I smiled right back. "Call me Jack," I said.

I figured I'd better get used to it, since I had decided to marry Alan. I didn't want kids. At least, not yet. But having someone to go home to after nights like that one was something I couldn't chance to pass up.

This case had changed me. Scared me. Matured me. Made me realize how strong I was, and what I was capable of. I had a new look. A new attitude. Soon I'd have a new rank.

And a new name would be perfect to go along with all of that.

Look out world, get ready for Jack Daniels.

Epilogue

He has waited for a while now.

Waited for the right moment.

The perfect time.

While he waited, he watched. And planned.

There was much planning.

Broken bones take time to heal. He wants Jack to be at her best.

It was actually a good thing to wait, because now Jack is having a baby.

The baby excites Luther. Jack has always been a fighter. Now she'll have even more to fight for. Even more to live for.

He's waited a long time.

He can wait a little longer.

Seven months, two weeks, and four days longer.

That's two days before Jack's due date.

Luther knows, because he found a nurse who worked for Jack's ob-gyn. He took the nurse to a nice, quiet spot, and she told him everything he wanted to know.

So he'll wait a bit longer.

Wait, and watch, and plan.

Wait until Jack's leg heals.

Wait until she's ready to have her baby.

That's when he will begin their game.

Author's Afterword

So you might have noticed that the end of *Shaken* appears to set up an eighth Jack Daniels novel involving Luther Kite, who actually isn't one of my characters.

Here's the story behind that.

I'm good friends with thriller author Blake Crouch, and our writing has covered many of the same themes of good and evil. I love his terror novels *Desert Places* and *Locked Doors*, which showcase his own unique, disturbing take on the serial killer genre.

In 2009, we wrote a novella together called *Serial Uncut* (available on Amazon), combining some of the characters from his work and my work, including Jack Daniels, Taylor (from *Afraid* and *Trapped*, written under my pen name, Jack Kilborn), and Mr. K. It also featured the villains from Blake's first two novels, specifically a fiendish maniac named Luther Kite.

I approached Blake with a simple, yet unique, idea: Wouldn't it be fun to take Jack and Luther and pit them against each other in a full-length novel? He was all for it. That novel is *Stirred*, which we're currently writing.

But aside from being just a fun collaboration where two writers go to war on the page, *Stirred* will also be something bittersweet for the authors. It will be the conclusion to my Jack Daniels series and the conclusion to Blake's Andrew Thomas series.

If you're new to my books, or Blake's books, and want to get caught up on the entire universe of these characters before reading *Stirred*, here is the order they go in, along with the characters they spotlight:

Shot of Tequila by J.A. Konrath (1991, Jack Daniels)

Desert Places by Blake Crouch (1996, Luther Kite)

Locked Doors by Blake Crouch (2003, Luther Kite)

Whiskey Sour by J.A. Konrath (2004, Jack Daniels, Alex Kork)

Bloody Mary by J.A. Konrath (2005, Jack Daniels)

Rusty Nail by J.A. Konrath (2006, Jack Daniels, Alex Kork)

Dirty Martini by J.A. Konrath (2007, Jack Daniels)

Serial Uncut by Blake Crouch, Jack Kilborn, and J.A. Konrath (1978–2010, Jack Daniels, Luther Kite, Taylor, Mr. K)

Afraid by Jack Kilborn (2008, Taylor)

Jack Daniels Stories by J.A. Konrath (2004–2010, Jack Daniels)

Fuzzy Navel by J.A. Konrath (2008, Jack Daniels, Alex Kork)

Cherry Bomb by J.A. Konrath (2009, Jack Daniels, Alex Kork)

Trapped by Jack Kilborn (2010, Taylor)

Shaken by J.A. Konrath (2010, Jack Daniels, Mr. K, Luther Kite)

Stirred by Blake Crouch and J.A. Konrath (2011, Jack Daniels, Luther Kite)

This may seem like a devious effort by us to get you to buy everything we've written. I swear it isn't. If it was, I would have mentioned Blake's novels *Abandon* and *Snowbound*, and my novels *Origin*, *Disturb*, *The List*, and *Endurance*. *The List* has a Jack Daniels cameo, and the heroes are Tom Mankowski and Roy Lewis, who have a bit part in *Shaken*.

Seriously, though. It really isn't necessary for you to read any of these previous novels to enjoy *Stirred*.

But we'd love you even more if you did. :)

Joe Konrath
Schaumburg, IL

Acknowledgments

I wish to thank everyone at D&G, especially Jane Dystel, Miriam Goderich, and Lauren Abramo.

The Amazon crew for their exceptional work, including Alex Carr, Stephanie Derouin, Terry Goodman, Victoria Griffith, Nader Kabbani, Jason Kuykendall, Brian Mitchell, Jeff Tollefson, Phil Finch, and Sarah Tomashek.

Blake Crouch, for too many things to mention.

Carl Graves, my brother from another mother.

My friends in high places, Barry Eisler, Tess Gerritsen, Heather Graham, Henry Perez, Kayla Perrin, Ann Voss Peterson, James Rollins, Marcus Sakey, Jeff Strand, Rob Walker, and F. Paul Wilson.

Talon Konrath, for tiptoeing around Dad when he was writing.

Maria Konrath, my everything. This book is for you, babe. But you wanna know a secret? They're all for you. I love you today.

And especially the fans, for the kind words, the e-mails, the reviews, the support, and the boundless enthusiasm for this series. You're the reason I keep writing.

Also, thanks to the beta readers/reviewers who read *Shaken* before it came out. If I missed your name, it's because you never e-mailed it to me or because I'm an idiot (probably the latter):

Melissa Zellmer, James Ross, Robert Junker, Catherine Saxton, Gretchen Rix, Sean Hicks, Stevie Ward, Susan Moblet, Lucille Brummett, Kevin McLaughlin, Darcia Helle, Jason Otoski, LaToya Morgan, Lawrence Zieminski, Jill McKelvey, S. Saldanha, Jennifer Golden, Cherie Reich, B. Waggoner, Jason Williams, J. Wilson, Paulette A. Brown, Cindy Chow, Anna Kahn, William Conner, Deborah Pendergast, Kathy Goryca, Sharon Baker, Cyntian B. Dempsey, Kathy Provost, Edward G. Talbot, Victoria Shipley, Travis Pierce, V.K. Browning, M. Pentico, David Dalton.

Author Biography

J.A. Konrath is the author of seven novels in the Lt. Jacqueline "Jack" Daniels thriller series, including *Whiskey Sour*, *Bloody Mary*, *Rusty Nail*, *Dirty Martini*, *Fuzzy Navel*, *Cherry Bomb*, and now *Shaken*. Writing under the name Jack Kilborn, he is the author of the horror novels *Afraid*, *Trapped*, and *Endurance*. He also writes sci-fi under the name Joe Kimball, whose novels are set in 2054 Chicago and feature Jack Daniels's grandson as the hero. To date, Konrath has sold over 100,000 e-books and has been featured in *Forbes*, the *Wall Street Journal*, and *Newsweek*. The author of more than seventy published short stories, he is the recipient of numerous writing awards and has seen his books published in eleven languages. He is currently at work on the final Jack Daniels novel, *Stirred*, co-written with Blake Crouch. You can visit him at JAKonrath.com.